THE SHERIDAN ROAD MYSTERY

PAUL AND MABEL THORNE

1st WORLD
LIBRARY
Literary Society

The Sheridan Road Mystery

Paul & Mabel Thorne

© 1st World Library – Literary Society, 2005
PO Box 2211
Fairfield, IA 52556
www.1stworldlibrary.org
First Edition

LCCN: 2004195656

Softcover ISBN: 1-4218-0477-8
Hardcover ISBN: 1-4218-0377-1
eBook ISBN: 1-4218-0577-4

Purchase *"The Sheridan Road Mystery"*
as a traditional bound book at:
www.1stWorldLibrary.org/purchase.asp?ISBN=1-4218-0477-8

1st World Library Literary Society is a nonprofit
organization dedicated to promoting literacy by:

- Creating a free internet library accessible from any computer worldwide.
- Hosting writing competitions and offering book publishing scholarships.

Readers interested in supporting literacy
through sponsorship, donations or
membership please contact:
literacy@1stworldlibrary.org
Check us out at: www.1stworldlibrary.ORG
and start downloading free ebooks today.

The Sheridan Road Mystery
contributed by Tim, Ed & Rodney
in support of
1st World Library Literary Society

CONTENTS

CHAPTER I

THE SHOT

It was a still, balmy night in late October. The scent of burned autumn leaves hung in the air, and a hazy moon, showing just over the housetops, deepened the shadows on, the streets.

Policeman Murphy stopped far a moment, as was his custom, at the corner of Lawrence Avenue and Sheridan Road. He knew that it was about two o'clock in the morning as that was the hour at which he usually reached this point. He glanced sharply up and down Sheridan Road, which at that moment seemed to be completely deserted save for the distant red tail-light of a belated taxi, the whir of whose engine came to him quite distinctly on the quiet night air.

JUST THEN POLICEMAN MURPHY HEARD A SHOT!

Instantly his body quickened with an awakened alertness, and he glanced east and west along the lonely stretch of Lawrence Avenue. He saw nothing, and concluded that the sound he had heard must have come from one of the many apartment buildings which surrounded him.

Murphy pondered for a moment. Was it a burglary, a domestic row, or perhaps a murder? The position of the shot was hard to locate, for it had been but the sound of a moment on the still night. Murphy, however, decided to take a chance, and started stealthily north on Sheridan Road, keeping within the shadow that clung to the buildings.

He had moved only a short distance in this way when a man in a bath robe dashed out of the doorway of an apartment house just ahead of him and ran north. Murphy instantly broke into pursuit. At the sound of his heavily shod feet on the pavement, the man in the bath robe stopped and turned. Murphy slowed up and the man advanced to meet him.

"I'm glad you're handy, Officer," panted the man. "I think somebody has been murdered in our building. Come and investigate."

"Sure," assented Murphy. "That's what I'm here for," and as they mounted the steps of the apartment house, he inquired, "What flat was it?"

"The top floor on the north side," replied the man, who then informed Murphy that his name was Marsh, and that he lived on the second floor, just below this apartment. "You see," Marsh continued, "a little while ago my wife and I were awakened by a noise in the apartment over us. It sounded like a struggle of some kind. As we listened we felt sure that several people were taking part in it. Suddenly there was a shot, and a sound followed as if a body had fallen to the floor. After that there was absolute silence. I hastily put on my bath robe, and was hurrying out to find a policeman when I met you."

By this time, Marsh, with Murphy at his heels, had reached the door of the third floor apartment. Murphy placed a thick forefinger on the button of the electric bell and rang it sharply several times. The men could distinctly hear the clear notes of the bell, but no other sound reached them. Again Murphy pressed the button without response.

"Murder, all right, I guess," muttered Murphy, "and the guy's probably slipped down the back stairs. Who lives here, anyway?" he inquired, turning to Marsh.

"That's the peculiar part about it," was the reply. "The people who rent this apartment went to Europe this summer, and as I understand it, they won't be back for another month. The apartment has been closed all summer. That is what amazed Mrs. Marsh and myself when we heard this sound above us."

"It looks like we'll have to break in," said Murphy. "Let me use your telephone."

"Certainly," agreed Marsh, and led the way to his apartment.

Murphy sat down at the telephone. His hand was on the receiver when he suddenly paused and turned to Marsh. "You know," he commented, half meditatively, "it's funny we haven't seen anybody else show up in the halls. I heard that shot way down at Lawrence Avenue. At least the people across the hall ought to have been waked up by it. Are you sure it was in this house?"

"Why certainly," retorted Marsh. "Didn't I tell you that we heard the struggle and the shot right over our heads?"

"Well, it sure takes a lot to disturb some people," said Murphy, as he placed the telephone receiver to his ear and called for his connection. After some words he got his precinct station.

"Hello!" he called. "Is that you, Sergeant? This is Murphy. I'm in the Hillcrest apartments on Sheridan Road. . . . Yes, that's right. . . . Just north of Lawrence Avenue. I think somebody's been murdered and we'll have to break in. Send the wagon, will you? . . . Don't know a damn thing yet," he added, evidently in reply to a question. "Hurry up the wagon." He replaced the receiver on its hook; then turned to Marsh as he stood up.

"I think I'll hang around the door up there until the boys come. Much obliged for your help. You'd better get back to bed now."

"Oh, no," objected Marsh. "I couldn't sleep with all this excitement going on. And then - Mr. Ames is a friend of mine. He would want me to look after things for him."

Murphy looked Marsh over in evident speculation. The man was tall and broad shouldered. His face was clean shaven. The features were strong, with a regularity that many people would consider handsome. He was what one would call a big man, but this appearance of bigness arose more from a heavy frame, and exceptional muscular development, than fleshiness. Murphy took in these details quickly, and the pause was slight before he spoke.

"Who's Ames?" he said.

"The man who rents the apartment upstairs." Then apparently taking the matter as settled, Marsh added, "I'll go along with you."

Murphy grunted, whether in assent or disapproval was hard to tell, but as he climbed the stairs again, Marsh was close beside him.

Murphy placed his hand on the doorknob and shook the door as he violently turned the knob. The door was securely locked. Then he threw his two hundred and some odd pounds against the door itself. The stout oak resisted his individual efforts.

"No use," he grumbled. "I'll have to wait 'till the boys come."

The two men then sat down on the top step to wait for the coming of the police. They chatted, speculating upon the possible causes of the disturbance. Marsh, however, seemed more interested in getting Murphy's ideas than in expressing opinions of his own. At length they heard the clang of the gong on the police patrol as it crossed Lawrence Avenue. They stood up expectantly. An instant later there was a clatter in the lower hall as the police entered. They mounted the stairs rapidly-two officers in uniform and another in civilian clothes.

"Where's the trouble?" cried the latter, as the party climbed the last flight.

"In here, as far as I know," returned Murphy, as he jerked a thumb over his shoulder toward the door of the apartment. "I can't get arise out of anybody. We'll have to break in."

Marsh stood aside while the four men took turns, two-and-two, in throwing themselves against the door. It creaked and groaned, and from time to time there was a sharp crack as the strong oak began to give.

In the meantime, the murmur of voices came up from the lower floors. Presently faces appeared on the landing just below where the police were working. Marsh leaned over the rail and in a few words outlined to the excited tenants what was going on.

Intent on their work of breaking in the door, the policemen paid little attention to their audience, and apparently did not notice that the door across the hall was still closed and silent. Murphy, however, recalled this fact later on.

At last, with a crash and a splintering of wood, the lock gave way and the door flew open. All was darkness and silence before them.

The five men stood grouped in the doorway, listening intently. The black silence remained unbroken save for the labored breathing of the men who had just broken in the door. The plain-clothes man then brought forth an electric pocket lamp and flashed its rays into the entrance hall, while the others drew their revolvers and held them in readiness. Then all stepped into the hallway. This was a large, square entrance way with four doorways opening from it. Two closed doors faced them. As they discovered later, these led to a bedroom, and the bathroom. The others, one opening toward the front of the apartment, and one toward the rear, were wide archways covered with heavy velvet portieres.

The plain-clothes man found the wall switch and turned on the electric light. Instructing one of his companions to watch the hall door, he led the others in a search of the apartment. Seeking for the electric light buttons as they moved about the apartment, the men soon flooded the rooms with light. Each man with revolver ready, and intent on searching every corner, none of them gave much attention to the fact that Marsh was dogging every move, apparently as keenly on the lookout as any one of the party.

Their inspection revealed nothing more than that the apartment was apparently in the same condition as its tenant had left it. The door to the outside stairway at the back was locked and the key was missing. In addition to the regular lock a stout bolt was in place. The catches on all the windows were properly locked, and all the shades remained drawn down close to the sills. It was an empty, locked apartment, with no outstanding evidence of having been used for a long time.

The police, now joined by the man lately on watch at the door, stood nonplussed in the kitchen. The plain-clothes man uttered an oath. Then he addressed his companions.

"I've seen some mighty fishy situations, but this trims anything I ever ran up against. Ain't been just hearing things, have you, Murphy? A swig of this home-made hootch does upset a man dreadful, sometimes."

Murphy glared.

"I ain't never touched the stuff," he bellowed. Then added, aggressively, "You know damned well I wasn't the only one to hear that shot. The tenant downstairs heard it, too. It was him that brought me in."

"Well, you only got his word for it that this is where the shot, was fired. Maybe HE'S trying to cover something up."

Murphy started, then glanced around.

"Hell!" he exclaimed. "Where's that guy gone to, anyway?"

Marsh, who had recently been close at their heels, was not now in the group. Murphy moved on tiptoe to the kitchen door and listened. On the other side of the dining room was the doorway to the entrance hall, and through the now drawn curtains this space was visible. Murphy could see that both these rooms were deserted, but an occasional swishing sound came to his ears. Turning to the waiting group, he silently and significantly jerked his head toward the front of the apartment. Following his example, they moved cautiously across the dining room and the hall and stopped at the door of the living room.

Marsh, with his back toward them, was just in the act of pulling a heavy, upholstered chair back into position. His moving of similar articles of furniture had made the sounds heard by Murphy.

Stepping suddenly into the room, Murphy inquired, with a note of sarcasm in his voice, "Kind of busy, ain't you?"

Marsh turned abruptly. If they expected to see any signs of confusion on his face they were disappointed, for he simply smiled cheerfully.

"Just following out a line of thought," he answered.

"What's the big idea!" asked the plain-clothes man, suspiciously, as he also stepped into the room and carefully looked over the man before him.

"Well, detectives in novels always search minutely for things which may not be apparent to the eye. When confronted with so deep a mystery as this one, I thought the application of a little of the story book stuff might do no harm."

"Huh!" snorted the plain-clothes man, as Marsh finished giving this information. "You're more than commonly interested in this affair, ain't you?"

"Naturally," agreed Marsh. "Remember, I live just below, and wouldn't like to be murdered in my bed some night. To hear a murder over your head is a bit disconcerting."

"How the devil do we know there's been a murder?" shot back the plain-clothes man. "We've only got your word for it."

"But this officer also heard the shot," and Marsh turned toward Murphy. "He was looking for the trouble when I met him."

"Yes," Murphy admitted. "I heard the shot, but I only got your word for it that it was here. If there was a murder, what became of the body?"

"That is for you gentlemen to find out," Marsh snapped back, now evidently alive to the fact that these men were regarding him with something approaching suspicion. "I have already done more than my share of the work. I have discovered visible proof THAT THERE WAS A MURDER!"

This information startled the group of policemen. Hasty glances swept the room for a moment. Then the plain-clothes man remarked, with a meaning smile, "Well, I'M from Missouri."

Marsh walked over to where the policemen stood.

"Take a look around," he began. "There are certain accepted ways of placing the furniture in a room. When there is a radical departure from such placing, an inquiring mind is led to wonder. Notice the chair I was just moving. It is located almost in the center of the room - obviously not its regular position. So why was it there?"

"Say, you'd make some detective!" came in an admiring tone from Murphy. The others nodded approval of the remark.

"I began to examine that chair and its surroundings carefully," continued Marsh, ignoring the interruption. He then moved over to the chair, and added, as he pulled it to one side, "I moved it away like this. Now, look at the floor!"

The policemen crowded forward. What Marsh had found was apparent at once. On the light background of the rug was a large, dark spot which the chair had covered. The plain-clothes man stooped and placed his hand on the spot. It felt damp to the touch, and as he stood erect again, holding his hand under the light, they all saw that the fingers were covered with a thin film of red.

"Blood!" cried Murphy.

"Yep," affirmed the plain-clothes man. "Fresh blood!"

Excited exclamations from the others showed their appreciation of the discovery.

Marsh smiled.

"I guess that looks like a possible murder," he said.

"The chair was placed there to cover the spot, all right," now admitted the plain-clothes man.

"But what became of the body?" again questioned Murphy.

"As I said before," Marsh answered him, "that is for you to find out. It is not my business."

"SOME mystery!" exclaimed the plain-clothes man. "This is a job for Dave Morgan."

CHAPTER II

DETECTIVE SERGEANT MORGAN

On Sheffield Avenue, just across from the ball park, where the "Cubs," Chicago's famous baseball team, has its headquarters, is a row of apartment houses. One realizes, of course, that these are not homes of wealth, but they have a comfortable, substantial look, which somehow conveys the idea that those who live there are good citizens, typical of the hard-working, progressive class that has made Chicago one of the greatest commercial cities of the world.

In one of these apartments lived Detective Sergeant Dave Morgan and his mother. He had located here in the days when, as a patrolman, he had walked beat out of the Town Hall Police Station, a short distance away. After his promotion to the detective force, he remained here because of the convenient location. The elevated railroad had its right of way directly back of his home, and the Addison Street station was only around the corner. He could quickly get to the Detective Bureau or almost any part of the widespreading city.

Morgan's home was unpretentious but comfortable. The hand of a careful and thoughtful housekeeper was in evidence everywhere. In the big living room, at the front, were several lounging chairs, and along one wall, between the front windows and the entrance door, stood two roomy bookcases. A glance at the titles showed the owner's inquiring and investigative turn of mind. His interest in his profession was also indicated by several volumes on criminology, and even popular detective stories of the day. In the center of the room was a commodious table with a large reading lamp. Beside the table was the big easy chair in which Morgan always sat, and where many of the solutions of difficult criminal problems had been worked out by him. Just across from this easy chair, and within reach of an outstretched hand, stood a tabouret, holding the telephone.

On the morning following the peculiar occurrence on Sheridan Road, Morgan was sitting in his favorite chair. His slippered feet were stretched before him and clouds of smoke hung about as he puffed at his favorite pipe, selected from a row of about ten that were hanging on a nearby home-made pipe holder. This might be said to be an eventful day for Dave Morgan. Only the day before, he and his partner, Detective Sergeant Tierney, had completed the solving of a baffling case and placed the criminal behind the bars. Now he had a well-earned and long-awaited "day off," and he was going to devote it to the restful pursuit of his favorite amusement - reading.

His mother, a white-haired, pleasant faced little woman, entered the room.

"Dave," she reminded him, "here's the morning paper. You forgot to look it over at breakfast."

"I know, Mother," he returned, "but I wanted to forget all about the world this morning. That Brock case has tired me out."

"But," she protested, "I notice from the headlines that there was a big murder on Sheridan Road last night. I didn't think you'd want to miss the details of that."

Professional instinct was too strong. Morgan reached for the paper and glanced quickly over the glaring headlines and the few words below, while the mother proudly watched him.

Morgan made a good figure for a detective. Not so tall as to be conspicuous, his breadth of shoulder and depth of chest clearly showed that he possessed the strength to meet most of the emergencies into which his work might lead him. His face had none of the hardened sharpness that usually marks the detective. In fact, although he was nearly thirty, his face still had a boyish look that made him appear younger, and taken with his sleek dark hair and mild brown eyes one would have presumed him to be just an average young business man rather than a hunter of criminals.

"No details here," he said, a moment later, laying the paper on the table. "They evidently received the notice just before going to press. Anyway, there is seldom much mystery about a murder. The men in that precinct probably have a line on who did it by this time."

"Yes, I know they use my boy only for the big cases," asserted the mother, and giving him an affectionate pat on the head, she went to her housework, while Morgan took a book from one of the cases, refilled his pipe, and settled down to spend a quiet morning in the big chair.

At eleven o'clock the telephone bell rang. Only a few words passed between Morgan and his caller, but the detective's face lighted up with interest. The instant he replaced the receiver he sprang to his feet, went to his bedroom, and hurriedly changed his clothes.

"Mother," he called. "The Chief has just 'phoned me that they have the biggest case for me that I ever handled. I must go down at once."

His mother came to the door of the room. "Can't you even wait for a bite of lunch?" she questioned.

"No," he explained, "it is a hurry call. The Chief says we cannot lose a minute in getting started. I'll have to stop in somewhere after I see the Chief."

Kissing his mother good-bye, Morgan hurried around to the elevated station. Fifteen minutes later he opened the Chief's office door.

"Sit down, Morgan," said the Chief, waving his hand toward a chair. "I've got a case here that'll make even you go some."

As Morgan sat down the Chief gathered up some typewritten sheets from his desk, and continued; "I didn't like to break up the first day you've had off in a long time, Morgan, but there was a murder on Sheridan Road last night - or early, this morning, to be exact – that has put a real mystery up to the Department. It'll need a man like you to solve it - if it can be solved. The newspapers had big headlines this morning, and the public will be watching us on account of the peculiar nature of the crime."

"I saw something about it in my paper this morning," said Morgan. "There were no details, however. The notice probably caught the last edition with little more than the fact that a murder had been committed."

"Well," exclaimed the Chief, "it's one of the biggest mysteries we've ever had handed to us. The shot was heard by both the man on the beat and a tenant in the building, but outside of the stories of these two men, and the discovery of a blood stain on a rug in a supposedly empty flat, not another thing has been found. The body is missing, and there is no trace of how it got out of the flat or where it is now. Here is a report of all that we know so far. By the way, your partner Tierney made this report. He happened to be on the job last night, so I told him to stick to it."

The Chief handed the typewritten sheets to Morgan.

"You will note," he went on, "that the man on beat heard a shot at about 2 A.M.; that he met a tenant from the house who said that he had heard sounds of a struggle, a shot, and something like the falling of a body. The police found the flat locked, and after they broke in could find no one on the premises. Nothing was upset, and there were no signs of the struggle, said to have taken place. Another peculiar thing is that the police even overlooked the bloodstain until the tenant who had heard the shot called their attention to it. Tierney tried to get some more details this morning, but you will find from his report that none of the other tenants admit hearing the shot; that the tenant in the flat across the hall was apparently not at home, and that the janitor says the people who rent the flat in which the trouble occurred, have been away all summer. The only really definite information of any kind comes from this one tenant, Marsh."

"You'll probably find Tierney at the flat, as I sent him back after he had turned in this report. He may have found out something more by now than he could put in that quick report."

"Chief," said Morgan, as he thumbed over the typewritten sheets in his hands, "you say there has been a murder committed here. With this tenant, Marsh, and a patrolman, getting into action so soon after the shot, a body couldn't possibly be moved out of the house - certainly, not without leaving some trace."

"Well?"

"How do we know there was a murder?"

"We don't know - positively," returned the Chief. "But we're not going to take any chances. Even if there wasn't an actual murder, SOMETHING OF A CRIMINAL NATURE WAS PULLED OFF IN THAT FLAT LAST NIGHT. What it was, we're putting up to you to find out. Go to it, Morgan! So long!"

CHAPTER III

INVESTIGATION

Leaving the Detective Bureau, Morgan stopped in a restaurant on Randolph Street for a quick lunch. From there he walked over to State Street and took the motor bus for the scene of the singular event which it was now his duty to investigate. A half-hour later he dropped off the bus at Lawrence Avenue and Sheridan Road. A few steps brought him to the Hillcrest apartments, where he found Tierney waiting on the front steps for him.

"The Chief telephoned me that you would probably be here about this time," said Tierney, after acknowledging Morgan's greeting. "I was on the job last night, and did a little investigating this morning, so the Chief thought you might want to talk things over with me."

Morgan nodded. "All right, let's go up. Can we get into the flat?"

"Sure," answered Tierney. "We put a temporary padlock on this morning, and I have the key."

Without further words the two men climbed the stairs to the apartment on the third floor. Tierney unlocked

Paul & Mabel Thorne

the padlock and they went in. Inside the entrance hall of the apartment, Tierney turned to Morgan.

"I suppose the Chief has put the case entirely in your hands, so it's up to you what you want to do first."

"We had better go into the front room here," answered Morgan, "and let me get a line on things. About all I know so far is that somebody THINKS a murder has been committed."

"You can't make much out of things as they are, that's a fact," assented Tierney, as they moved into the front room. He dropped into an easy chair close at hand, and pushed his cap back on his head, while Morgan went to one of the front windows and ran the shade to the top. Seating himself where he could get the full benefit of the light from the window, he drew out the typewritten report and read it over carefully.

"This is your report, isn't it, Tierney?" he inquired, folding up the sheets again and replacing them in his pocket.

"You bet; and I put into it every damned thing I know," asserted Tierney. "And that's mighty little," he added. "This is the most mysterious case I ever saw."

There was a pause while Morgan drew a pipe from his pocket and filled and lighted it. Then settling back in his chair, he looked at Tierney. "Got any theories?" he asked.

"No," replied Tierney. "I haven't any theories - but I've got a couple of suspicions."

"Well?"

"One," continued Tierney, "is this flat across the hall. Murphy - that's the man on the beat who heard the shot and investigated - Murphy noticed that in spite of all the racket we made breaking down the door last night, no one in that flat showed any interest. I tried to get in touch with them this morning. Nothing doing. Either they weren't home, or wouldn't answer the bell."

"That looks bad," commented Morgan. "You mentioned in your report that you talked with the janitor. Did he drop anything about them that you didn't think worth while putting in the report?"

"The janitor simply told me that a man and his daughter lived in the flat, and that he thought the man was away a good deal; so he supposed he must be a traveling man. They have always seemed to be quiet people. He has never even seen them have any company." "That's suspicious, too," declared Morgan. "Normal people usually have SOME company. Is that all?"

Tierney nodded.

"Now," prompted Morgan, "you said you had another suspicion."

"You bet!" exclaimed Tierney, straightening up in his chair. "That guy, Marsh - underneath here."

"'Great minds'," laughed Morgan. "I sort of focused on that man myself after reading your report just now."

"Well, here's the way I look at it," explained Tierney.

"When ordinary folks hear fighting and shooting in the middle of the night, they generally stick their heads under the covers and lie close. They don't put on bath robes and run out on the street to be the first to give a report. Then the janitor tells me that he's seen this man around a lot in the daytime - 'no visible means of support,' you might say. Both Murphy and I remember that Marsh referred to his wife. The janitor says he's pretty sure that he never saw any woman around the flat. And when I asked Marsh this morning to let me talk to his wife, he said she was not in."

"You probably noticed in my report that it was this Marsh who showed us the bloodstain under the chair. You know, we came out of the kitchen and caught that guy in the act of pulling a chair over the spot. He said he was replacing the chair where he found it. I've been wondering whether he wasn't actually covering up the spot himself. When we caught him in the act, maybe he just decided to bluff it out."

"The Department didn't make any mistake when they shifted you into the Detective Bureau, Tierney," said Morgan, laughing. "Has the Chief assigned you to any other case for my day off?"

"No," replied Tierney. "When the Chief told me to come back and meet you here I figured he wanted me to stick to this case with you."

"So I thought," agreed Morgan. "But I want to be left alone here for awhile. You scout around and see if you can find out something more about this tenant across the hall. Do you know his name?"

"Clark Atwood, it says on the mail box downstairs."

"All right, Tierney. See what you can look up in this neighborhood. I'll get in touch with you later. By the way, you had better leave that key with me."

Tierney handed over the key to the padlock, and with a cheery "So long," started off.

Morgan, left to himself, began a careful inspection of the apartment. Although assured that the apartment had been unoccupied, his first act was to discover, if possible, any signs of recent habitation. Convinced by the blood spot that the principal part of whatever had happened had taken place in the front room, he decided to leave that room until the last. Running all the shades to the top of the windows as he passed from the front to the rear of the apartment, Morgan made the place as light as possible. He began his examination with the kitchen. The fastenings on the windows were closed, and the undisturbed condition of the dust indicated that they had not been touched for a long period. A careful inspection of the glass and woodwork showed no finger marks or any attempt to open the catches. The bolt on the back door was unfastened, but as the report stated that the police had found this bolt in place, it was obvious that it had simply been left open by the police. Morgan carefully scrutinized the condition of the bolt. After pushing it back into place the difference in brightness of the protected and unprotected parts convinced him that the bolt had been closed for some time.

He also noted that the key was missing from the lock. However, this fact had been referred to in the report, and it could make little difference if the bolt itself had been fastened. As a matter of fact, during his search of the pantry, he discovered the key on top of the ice box.

A layer of dust indicated that the key had not been touched for a long time. His thorough investigation of the pantry revealed no evidence of recent use. The ice box was dry as a bone, with the musty smell of long disuse. A touch of the finger on various dishes and pieces of glassware showed that these also were covered with a film of dust.

Before leaving the kitchen, Morgan glanced into the sink, to ascertain if, as often happens, the murderer had washed his hands there. There was a reddish stain about the outlet, but as Morgan found this covered with dust her surmised that a long time had elapsed since any water had been run in the sink. This stain was presumably the rust which usually gathers in a long unused sink or basin.

The small maid's room off the kitchen had certainly not been in use. Only the bare mattress was on the bed, and Morgan noticed that as his own feet left imprints in the dust on the floor, it was not likely that anyone else could have been in the room without leaving similar traces.

Next he thoroughly searched the dining room. As this room usually seems to be the favorite gathering point, both for the occupants of a house and unbidden prowlers, Morgan's keen eyes examined every detail of the floor and furnishings, including the drawers of the sideboard. He immediately noticed that two of the chairs were standing close to the table, while two others were moved slightly back from the table as if people had been sitting in them. On the floor under one of these chairs he found a few spots of cigarette ashes. To Morgan's quick mind this carried a mental picture. Of course, the police who had been in the apartment the night before might have accidentally or intentionally moved the chairs, but he was quite sure that under the circumstances not one of them would have sat down to smoke a cigarette. At some time quite recently, therefore, somebody, probably two persons, had sat at this dining room table while conversing, or waiting for something.

This was further confirmed when Morgan, bending his knees and lowering his body so as to bring his eyes on a level with the table, studied the top in the reflected light. He saw that the dust on the table top had been disturbed in front of the two chairs. Furthermore, he discovered that the person who had not be smoking had evidently rested a pair of clasped and sweaty hands on the table top, as two parallel, greasy marks, made by the sides of the hands, showed quite plainly. To Morgan, clasped and sweaty hands indicated a possible state of nervousness. Either this had been the victim or the chief plotter.

The dining room revealed nothing further to Morgan, but he felt that he had made some progress in establishing the fact that at least two people had quite recently been in this supposedly unoccupied apartment.

Passing through the entrance hall, Morgan then examined the main bedroom, which opened off of it. The bed had been dismantled, as in the maid's room. An examination of the clothes closet, and the drawers of the dresser and a chiffonier, showed that the room was commonly occupied by a man and a woman. Everything quite obviously belonged to the regular tenant. Morgan could find nothing of a suspicious nature, although he had particularly looked for correspondence which might in some indefinite way connect this tenant with the happenings of the night before.

The bathroom was visited next. Outside of the usual toilet articles and harmless medical "first aids" in the cabinet, the room was bare.

The final step was a close examination of the front room. Here the blood spot stood out dark and forbidding in the light of the afternoon sun. Beyond the fact that the shot had taken effect, it told nothing. Morgan stood in thought with his eyes resting upon the brick fireplace. Suddenly the descending sun threw its rays farther into the room and rested on a bright spot at the side of the fireplace. It looked odd to Morgan and he approached it. What he found was a flattened bullet, which had been held in place by slightly embedding itself in the rough surface of the brick. As evidence it had small value outside of confirming the fact that a shot had been actually fired in this apartment.

Finding nothing else with a bearing on the case, Morgan started to leave. At the doorway to the entrance hall, he stopped and turned to take one last look around the room in the hope that something might suggest itself. As he stood making this last survey, his eye caught a faint point of light under a cabinet in a corner. Instantly he returned to the room, and stooping down, ran his hand under the cabinet. His fingers seized on a small object, which proved to be a gold cuff button. As he turned it over in his hand he found the initial "M" deeply engraved in the heavy gold.

Remembering that he had learned from the report in his pocket that the name of the tenant of this apartment was Ames, this discovery immediately assumed great importance, so Morgan carefuly placed the cuff button in a vest pocket.

Encouraged by his find, Morgan made another careful examination of the room. The flattened bullet and the cuff button, revealed by friendly rays of sunlight, seemed to be all that he could find.

Paul & Mabel Thorne

CHAPTER IV

THE APARTMENT ACROSS THE HALL

After replacing the padlock and snapping it closed, Morgan pressed the electric button of the apartment across the hall. Footsteps sounded in immediate response, and the next moment the door was furtively opened. Morgan, who by that time was leaning carelessly against the jamb, quietly moved one foot forward into the opening.

Although the light in the hallway was dim he could see that the woman who stood there was young and remarkably pretty. Removing his hat, he asked politely, "Are you the tenant here?"

"Yes," came in a soft but nervous voice.

"May I come in and talk with you a few minutes?" inquired Morgan.

"What is it you want?" the girl inquired.

Morgan threw back his coat and disclosed his badge. "I am a city detective, and I would like a few words with you about this affair across the hall."

"What affair is that?" asked the girl.

Morgan smiled. "Didn't you know there was some trouble across the hall last night?"

"No," she returned. "I retired early and have heard nothing about it."

Morgan was at a loss for a moment. The girl was not of the type that one would associate with persons of a criminal sort. Her replies had been given in a tone of voice so candid and wondering that it hardly seemed possible she could be acting. Whatever the situation, however, Morgan wanted to get inside this apartment and study the girl more closely.

"Well, I'll tell you all about it," he said, gently, "if you'll let me come in for a moment or two."

"I know nothing about it," she maintained, with a touch of irritation in her voice, and Morgan's foot signaled to him that she was attempting to close the door.

Morgan never liked to be rough in his methods. He hesitated over forcing himself into the presence of this young woman, and yet he now had an impression that an interview with her was imperative. There was a slight pause, as he ran over in his mind some way to gain his entrance without force.

"Do you know Mr. Marsh downstairs?" he inquired, suddenly, his eyes keeping a keen watch on her face.

"I do not know any of the tenants in the building."

"That's strange," said Morgan, thoughtfully. "I was just talking with Mr. Marsh, and he told me that you knew all about the trouble last night. He suggested that if I would come and see you I could get just the information I wanted."

"I don't know this Mr. Marsh, and I can't understand why he should make such a statement." Surprise was apparent in her voice.

Morgan was quite sure that her surprise was genuine. At the same time his remarks had just the effect he had hoped they would. It brought a new element into the matter and added to the girl's natural curiosity. She opened the door wider, and nodding toward the front room, said, "Step in and tell me what you wish to know."

The room into which Morgan entered was a counterpart of the one across the hall, though as he rapidly observed the furnishings, he was impressed with the greater taste displayed and the homelike atmosphere. A piece of embroidery, on which she had evidently been working, lay on the arm of a chair near the window.

Conjecturing that she would resume her seat in this chair, Morgan seated himself where he could keep his back to the window, while the girl whom he was about to question would directly face the full light. Morgan's guess was correct. The girl went directly to the chair she had left to answer his ring, and taking up her embroidery, picked nervously at its edges, meanwhile watching Morgan expectantly.

Surmising that a direct attempt to question her at once might defeat his purpose, Morgan immediately broke into an account of the previous night's occurrence. As he brought out the various details of what was reported to have taken place, he slyly watched her face. At the end of his recital, he felt convinced that what he told the girl had previously been unknown to her. Moreover, Morgan became sensible of a growing feeling of interest and confidence in the girl. Her sweetness seemed so genuine, her dark blue eyes so frank and honest in the straightforward way they met his.

"It seems very strange that I heard none of the excitement," remarked the girl, when Morgan had finished his story. "I had a rather busy day yesterday with my studies and retired early."

Morgan had decided upon his line of questioning while relating the incidents of the night before.

"May I ask your name?"

"Certainly," she replied. "My name is Atwood."

Morgan, having noticed the absence of a wedding ring, assumed that she was unmarried. Therefore, he said, "Is your mother at home, Miss Atwood?"

A shade of sadness passed over her face. "My mother died some months ago," she replied.

"I am sorry. I know what it is to have a good mother," sympathized Morgan. Then he inquired, "Perhaps your father heard the disturbance?"

"Oh no," she replied. "My father is away."

"He travels?"

"Yes; my father is a salesman."

"For some Chicago house, I suppose."

"No; for a business house in St. Louis. We formerly lived there."

"St. Louis is a pleasant city," commented Morgan. "Still, many people prefer Chicago."

"Oh, I think I should prefer to live in St. Louis, because I have a few friends there," she said. "But I am studying music, and when my mother died, father suggested that I live in Chicago where I could attend a better musical college. Then, too, father could get home more often as he travels in this vicinity."

"I suppose your father travels for some well known St. Louis house?" suggested Morgan.

"Well, really, I don't know the name of his firm," returned the girl. "Business has never held any interest for me."

It struck Morgan as strange that even a girl who did not take an interest in business should be ignorant of the name of the firm by whom her father was employed, yet he seemed to find many things that were contradictory in this girl. The chatty line of conversation he had taken was bringing out information in a manner highly satisfactory to Morgan. He was about to make another comment, that might elicit further facts, when he was interrupted by a question which he had been expecting.

"Tell me," inquired Miss Atwood, a slight color

coming to her cheeks, "what this man Marsh said about me."

Morgan was pleased. This gave him an opening for some questioning which he had hesitated to take up before. He wanted to know just how much this girl knew about Marsh. "Don't you really know Mr. Marsh?" he began.

"No," she replied. "I didn't even know there was such a person in the house."

"Well, that is certainly strange. I'm sure that he told me to talk to the young lady on the top floor. Perhaps he meant some young lady who lived across the hall. Still, there doesn't seem to have been anyone there since the trouble."

Miss Atwood smiled. "He could not have meant anyone in that apartment, for I understand it is occupied only by an elderly couple, a Mr. Ames and his wife. I understood father to say that he had heard they were traveling in Europe. I am sure no one has lived there since we have been in this apartment."

"How long have you been here?" asked Morgan.

"Let me see," said Miss Atwood, thoughtfully. "This is almost the end of October, and we have been here since the middle of July. That is a little over three months, isn't it?"

"July," repeated Morgan. "That isn't a renting season. You must rent this apartment furnished."

"We do," she replied, promptly. "Father was too busy

to spend any time on moving, so we stored our things in St. Louis and took this apartment."

"Real estate agents have been making lots of money these days. I hear a great many people have to pay them a bonus for finding apartments. I suppose they stuck you that way, too."

"No," returned the girl. "I understand that father rented direct from the tenant. I believe the tenant was a friend of his, or someone he knew in a business way."

The embroidery which had been lying in Miss Atwood's lap had gradually slipped forward and at this moment dropped to the floor. As she reached down to pick it up, Morgan's alert eyes noted a purplish mark on her forearm.

"You seem to have bruised your arm, Miss Atwood," he said, in a tone that was intended to express sympathy.

"Oh, did you notice that mark?" she exclaimed. "That has been puzzling me all day. I awoke suddenly last night with a feeling as if something had bitten me, but almost immediately went to sleep again. During the morning I noticed this mark and the swelling. I can't imagine what could have done it."

"May I look at it?" asked Morgan, as he rose and approached her. "Perhaps I can suggest something."

She extended her arm, and Morgan, taking her hand, drew the arm close to him. He carefully studied the spot. The only time he had ever seen such marks before was on the arms of drug addicts who had not been particularly careful in the application of the hypodermic needle.

"So you think it is a bite of some kind?" asked Morgan, looking keenly at her.

"I can't imagine what else it could be," she replied.

Morgan dropped her hand and looked out of the window for a moment. There was no doubt in his mind that the mark had been made by a hypodermic needle, yet it was the only mark of the kind that he could see on her arm, and therefore would hardly seem to indicate that the girl was a drug fiend. Moreover, there had bean no indication of embarrassment or nervousness in her reference to the mark, as would undoubtedly have been the case had she been addicted to the use of a drug. Morgan realized, too, that the fresh pink and white skin of this girl, and the bright eyes, could not be maintained if drugs were taken. The case was growing more puzzling every minute. Had the use of a hypodermic needle on this girl anything to do with the supposed tragedy across the hall?

After this discovery, Morgan hesitated to ask further questions at this time, so he turned to the girl again and remarked, simply, "It is possible that some kind of spider bit you in the night. If you have any peroxide in the house, I would suggest that you bathe the spot with it. And now I must be going. If I have your permission, Miss Atwood, I would like to drop in again sometime to let you know about any further discoveries I may make on this case."

"Thank you," she returned. "I shall be interested."

As he turned to say good-bye at the door, she added, apologetically, "I am sorry I had no information to give you."

"Oh, that's all right," Morgan assured her, "I appreciate your courtesy in letting me have this little chat with you." But as he drew the door to after him, Morgan smiled and said to himself, "Poor little girl; you don't realize what a lot of information you have given me."

CHAPTER V

PECULIAR FACTS

When Morgan reached the second floor on his way down, he paused a moment before Marsh's door. So far as he had gone in this case, Morgan was confronted with two factors; the connection of this man with the case, and the bearing which Miss Atwood and her father might have upon it. Without doubt, some singular conditions surrounded the Atwoods, but his knowledge of these was still too vague to give him even a basis for reasoning. On the other hand, the questionable circumstances surrounding the connection of this man Marsh with the case, were very definite, indeed, and though Morgan tried to avoid hasty conclusions, he could not keep back his growing suspicions of Marsh. As he hesitated before Marsh's door, Morgan thought that it moved slightly. Stepping closer and pushing the door gently with an outstretched hand, he found it tightly closed. Yet, he had a feeling that the door had been softly closed after he had stopped on the landing. That decided Morgan. The time was not opportune for an interview with this man. He wanted to obtain some additional facts before taking the step he was now convinced would have to be taken, and so went on down the stairs to carry his investigations further.

Leaving the house, Morgan turned the corner of Lawrence Avenue and entered the alleyway in the rear of the Hillcrest apartments.

Practically all Chicago apartment houses have an outside rear stairway for the use of tradespeople. Usually, this stairway is open so that anything which takes place can be observed from all nearby houses. In this instance the stairway was enclosed, with a door leading to the back porch of each apartment. A person could pass from the alley up to the third floor without being noticed, even by tenants in the building itself.

Morgan instantly noted that an automobile could stand in the alleyway close to the entrance; that a person could come down these stairs unobserved, step into the car and be quietly carried away, disappearing into the general traffic of the streets in probably not more than two minutes after leaving the apartment.

Here, thought Morgan, was a possible solution of the sudden disappearance of the person who had been either murdered or wounded. It was a problem, of course, as to which door they had been brought through, and the solution of that problem would very likely bring him pretty close to the person or persons who had participated in the events of the night before.

Unquestionably, the rear door of the apartment where the trouble had taken place had not been used for this purpose, although it would seem the logical and quickest way to make an exit. On the other hand, for that very reason, the persons back of the supposed crime had been clever enough to avoid it, thus adding a mystifying element to what had taken place.

In the light of present developments, two possible exits suggested themselves to Morgan. These were the Atwood and Marsh apartments. The girl, however, claimed that she had slept through the night, and it hardly seemed possible that anyone could pass through her flat without arousing her. This, of course, meant taking for granted her story that she was alone in the apartment and had been in bed and sleeping. While Morgan felt attracted toward the girl, and placed considerable confidence in her honesty, he did not allow these emotions to entirely dull his sense of suspicion. If things did not clear themselves shortly he would carry his investigations further along this line.

In the meantime, his distrust centered on the Marsh apartment. This man admitted being awake during the reported struggle, and there was no question about his being partly dressed and in action while some of the events were taking place. Marsh could easily have passed a person or a body to a confederate through his back door, locked the door and then hurried into Sheridan Road to direct the attention of the police, or any other persons who had been aroused, to the front of the house, thus enabling his confederate to get quietly, safely and quickly away. This was only bare theory on Morgan's part. He needed definite facts to either confirm this theory, or to prove that his judgment was at fault. The cuff button, with its initial "M," looked curiously like one of these facts, and, taken in connection with the other circumstances, pointed strongly toward Marsh.

He wanted to know more about Marsh, and the girl had given him some basic facts which would enable him to enlarge his fund of information. The owner, or the real estate agent who managed the building, seemed to be the logical starting point for securing this information. To find out the names of these people must be his next step.

Luckily, at this moment the janitor of the apartment building appeared, rolling a barrel of ashes up from the basement. While it was quite obvious that such was the case, Morgan opened the conversation by inquiring, "Are you the janitor of this flat house?"

"Yes, sir," replied the man.

"Does the owner run this building, or has he placed an agent in charge?"

"A real estate agent manages it," the janitor informed him. "Parker Cole - over on Broadway."

"Thanks," said Morgan, and returned down the alley to Lawrence Avenue where he turned west and walked over to Broadway. A few minutes later he stood at the counter in the real estate office, and a man approached him.

"Is either Mr. Parker or Mr. Cole in?"

"I am Mr. Cole," announced the man. "What can I do for you?"

Morgan opened his coat a minute to give Cole a glimpse of his badge; then said, "I would like to talk confidentially with you for a few minutes."

"Step into my private office," directed Cole, opening a gate as he spoke, and indicating a space partitioned off at the rear.

"What is the trouble?" he inquired, when they were seated.

"I came to see you in connection with the trouble in the Hillcrest last night."

"A most unfortunate affair!" exclaimed Cole. "It is the first time anything of the kind ever occurred in any of the buildings under our management. It is most unfortunate," he repeated.

"I have been assigned to the case," Morgan informed him, "and I am gathering all the information possible. Then I can formulate some theory upon which to work. Just at this time I want a little information regarding your tenants in the building."

"Very fine people - very fine people, indeed," protested Cole. "There couldn't be a breath of suspicion against any of them."

"I'll be the judge of that," said Morgan, sharply.

"But really," cried Cole, "you must not annoy our tenants. Surely it was only a quarrel among burglars. One man probably wounded his pal and then, alarmed at the disturbance he had created, hurried him away."

Morgan smiled. This was a very ingenious and plausible solution of the mystery - at least in the real estate agent's eyes. However, Morgan now sought facts, not amateur theories, and disregarding the real estate man's talk, he pushed his quest for information.

"I have a report in my pocket which covers all that I want to know about most of your tenants; at least for

Paul & Mabel Thorne

the present. There are two families, however, about whom I want further information. The first is the Atwood family, in the third floor south."

"Atwood - Atwood," repeated Cole, as if he did not place the name. Then he called, "Joe, bring me the rent book."

Morgan became alert. It was possible that a man like Cole, with a large list of properties under his management, might be somewhat vague in his recollection of the names of a few of his tenants. This case was different. The Atwoods, according to the girl's story, had sub-leased their apartment quite recently, presumably with the agent's sanction. The present excitement should naturally have recalled this matter to Cole's mind - should even have concentrated his thoughts upon the names and characteristics of every tenant in this particular building. Cole's unfamiliarity with the name of Atwood, therefore, seemed peculiar.

At this moment a boy entered with a large volume. Laying it on Cole's desk, the boy passed quietly out of the office. Cole glanced at the index and then turned over certain pages in the book.

"We have no Atwood in that house," he declared, finally, looking up at Morgan. "You must have made a mistake."

Before replying, Morgan pulled out a small notebook and spread it open on his knee, ready for use. He also extracted a pencil from his vest pocket. Glancing at the point to see that it was in working condition, he turned to Cole with the question, "Who does occupy the third floor south in that house?"

"A family named Crocker."

"Full name, please."

"Joseph Crocker. He rented that apartment one year ago the first of this month," stated Cole, after further reference to the book.

Morgan jotted this down in his notebook.

"You haven't heard that Mr. Crocker sub-leased his flat?" inquired Morgan.

"No," replied Cole, positively. "I would be sure to know about it, too. A transaction of that kind must be put through and reported in this office."

"Can you give me any further particulars about Mr. Crocker?"

"Well, of course, I could look up his references and the other papers, if you wish me to. But as I recall it, he came from St. Louis and had excellent references from that city."

"I won't bother you to look anything more up on that just now," said Morgan. "I may be interested in the information later. I'll see what I can find out first."

"How did you come to associate the name of Atwood with that apartment?" inquired Cole.

"I thought that was the name mentioned in the report I have. It was probably a mistake of the man who first went through the building. They often make mistakes in names," Morgan added, reassuringly, as it was not his desire to start Cole on any investigation of his own at this time. "Now, what can you tell me about the Marsh family, second floor north? "

"Well, there's a party I can tell you more about. It made an impression upon me at the time we rented the apartment, because we had to make special arrangements."

"Yes," said Morgan, encouragingly.

"You see," continued Cole, "owing to a death in the family, the people who occupied that apartment moved out in July, and I sublet the apartment for them from the first of August, to a Mr. Gordon Marsh. Mr. Marsh, I understand, was driven off his ranch in Mexico by the revolutionists. As he knew practically no one in the United States to whom he could refer, we finally compromised by his agreeing to pay his rent quarterly in advance."

"How much of a family has he?" asked Morgan.

"Only his wife," returned Cole. "That was one reason we were willing to come to terms with him. We like small families; like Mr. Ames, who rents the apartment where this trouble occurred."

Morgan welcomed this mention of Ames. It gave him an opening for further questions regarding this tenant. He was not overlooking the fact that the Ames family might in some way be connected with the affair.

"I suppose Mr. Ames and his wife are still away?" he inquired.

"Yes," returned Cole. "We received his October rent through his London bankers, White, Wyth, Harding; and only a few days ago, a letter referring to some decorating to be done when he returns next month. By the way, why are you particularly interested in these families?"

"Just happen to be people we didn't get reports on at the building, that is all. Our reports on a case of this kind have to be complete."

"Quite right - quite right," approved Cole, his curiosity evidently satisfied.

"Mr. Marsh and Mr. Ames are friends, are they not?" queried Morgan, casually, as he noted down in his book what Cole had recently told him.

"Not so far as I know. In fact, it hardly could be possible, inasmuch as Mr. Ames and his wife went abroad before Mr. Marsh arrived in Chicago."

CHAPTER VI

THE CABLE FROM LONDON

After leaving the real estate office, Morgan walked south on Broadway to Wilson Avenue and entered the Western Union office. Here he sent a short cable to London. Leaving his address so that the reply could be forwarded to him, he went across the street and took an elevated train for home.

After dinner Morgan settled down in his favorite chair to await Tierney, who had telephoned that he would be there in a little while. As he was filling his pipe for the second time, the bell rang. Morgan opened the door and Tierney bustled in. The cheerful smile, the snappy step, and the careless motion with which Tierney shot his hat into a nearby chair, told Morgan as plainly as words, that his partner brought worth while information. Tierney pulled an easy chair up to the table, and Morgan pushed the tobacco jar and an extra pipe over to him. Tierney filled the pipe, lighted up, and settling back, grinned at Morgan.

"I may have exceeded orders, but I've sure got some dope on that guy, Marsh. You told me to find out what I could about Atwood. I visited various stores in the neighborhood which a family was likely to patronize. No one knew the name. After I had stopped in a cigar store, and found that his name was not in the telephone directory, I figured that there was nothing more I could do along that line until I'd talked things over with you. So I decided to hang around in sight of the house and watch developments."

"At a quarter to three a young woman came out, walked down to Lawrence Avenue and stood on the corner, apparently waiting for a motor bus. As she did not look like anyone I had seen in the house, I gave her the once-over."

"Was she about medium height, slender, with blonde hair and dark blue eyes?" questioned Morgan.

"Well, I didn't get close enough to gaze fondly into her eyes," said Tierney, "but the rest of your description fits all right. Do you know who she is?"

"Probably Miss Atwood," Morgan explained, "daughter of the tenant in the flat across the hall. In the future it will do no harm to keep one eye on her, Tierney."

"I kept both eyes on her today, Morgan, and that's the way I got the dope I did."

Morgan smiled appreciatively, and Tierney went on.

"As I was saying, I watched this girl as she waited for the bus. Suddenly I glanced toward the house, and there was this guy, Marsh, standing just inside the doorway. To me it looked as if he was trying to keep an eye on this girl, without her seeing him if she looked back. So I kept out of sight as far as I could and watched the two of them. Sure enough, in about one minute along comes the bus and the girl gets in. Would you believe it, Morgan, that very minute Marsh dashes across the street, nails an empty taxi and starts after the bus."

"Now, I ain't as quick as you, Morgan, but I sure figured that my cue was to join the procession. Luck was with me, for the minute I got this idea I spotted a Checker taxi and rushed at it so hard the driver nearly fainted. 'Follow that Yellow ahead!' I yelled to the driver, and before he came to a full stop I had jumped in and we were off."

"We trailed down Sheridan Road, through Lincoln Park, and on to Michigan Avenue - the girl in the bus, Marsh in the Yellow, and me in the Checker. Just after we passed Adams Street the Yellow stopped at the curb and Marsh got out. I stopped my cab quick, and as I saw that Marsh was paying off his driver, I settled with mine and got ready for the next move."

"Marsh started down Michigan Avenue, and I could keep pretty close on account of the crowd. Pretty soon I sighted this girl trotting along a little way ahead of us. Now, there's a situation for you, Morgan - Marsh trailing the girl and me trailing Marsh."

At this point Morgan's interest was shown by the fact that he sat forward in his chair with his elbows on his knees, and for the moment forgot to pull at his pipe.

Tierney continued. "The girl turns into a building at six hundred and something Michigan Avenue - I've got the exact number in my book. Marsh strolls over to the curb, while I, taking advantage of his back being turned for the moment, shot into the building after her. She entered an elevator, and I strolled in, too. Luckily, she stood near the door, so I could get into the back of the car and not be specially noticed. She got off at a musical school. As we had been the only two people in the elevator, I took a chance, and said to the man running it, 'Some looker!'"

"'Yes,' he says, 'a fine looking girl. She comes here twice a week.'"

"'Well,' says I, 'that's a good thing for women - to learn music. How long do they teach them?'"

"'You mean, how long does a lesson last?' he asked me."

"'Yes,' I told him."

"'Oh, about a half-hour,' he says. 'Say! What floor do you want?' he shot at me as he reached the top."

"'Good Lord!' I says, winking at him. 'That dame sure upset me. I want to go back two floors.'"

"When he let me out I hustled over to the stairway, went down to the ground floor, and when Marsh had his eyes turned away for a minute, I beat it out and up Michigan."

"Now, Morgan, here's where I was clever. That girl was good for a half-hour and so was Marsh, if he was following her; as I was pretty sure he was. Now you or I haven't seen all of the inside of Marsh's apartment, have we? And yet we suspect this guy, and want to get something on him if we can."

Morgan nodded, and began to smile as he gathered what Tierney was about to tell him.

"Well, Morgan, I figured that a half-hour would give me all the time I needed, so I ran over to the elevated and went back to Lawrence Avenue. I slipped up the alleyway, back of the house, and climbed the rear stairs to Marsh's flat. After thumping on the door several times I made sure no one was home, especially as the shades in the kitchen and the pantry were pulled down. So I pulled out my bunch of keys and had the luck to find one that opened the lock. I closed the door softly, and tiptoed through the kitchen and the dining room. Would you believe it, Morgan - THERE WASN'T A STICK OF FURNITURE IN THOSE ROOMS!"

"You mean the place was empty?" asked Morgan.

"Up to the entrance to the hallway it was absolutely bare, Morgan. The living room is furnished, and so is the bedroom; and there were a few toilet articles in the bathroom. He has a pair of heavy drapes across the doorway to the dining room, so that anyone coming in would never guess the back part wasn't furnished. I looked things over pretty carefully in the few minutes I had, and I didn't find a single article that belonged to a woman. I tell you, Morgan, that fellow's living there alone and only got half the flat furnished! Take it from me, he's got something on. That flat's just a blind. If it was me, I'd lock him up tonight."

"Well, it's coming pretty soon, Tierney," acceded Morgan. "What you've found out today will help a lot."

There was a few minutes pause as the two men smoked their pipes, and Morgan analyzed the facts which

Tierney had given him. Suddenly he leaned over and picked up the telephone from the tabouret.

"What's doing?" exclaimed Tierney.

"We shouldn't leave that man Marsh unwatched from now on," explained Morgan.

"I know it, Morgan, and I've taken care of all that."

"You mean the house is watched?"

"Sure," said Tierney. "The minute I got out of the flat this afternoon I telephoned the captain of the precinct and told him just enough to get his co-operation. There's a man on the job now and he won't leave there, unless he follows Marsh, until I relieve him in the morning."

"There's one drawback to that," observed Morgan, as he set the telephone back in place. "No one knows Marsh except you."

"There's a man knows him better than I do - Murphy, the man on the beat. He spent quite a spell with Marsh last night."

"That's right," agreed Morgan. "How did you fix it?"

"The Captain put another man on Murphy's beat, and put Murphy into plain-clothes for tonight. It worked all right, because Murphy was a night man anyway."

"You're all right, Tierney," Morgan complimented him.

Tierney grinned his appreciation.

"Now then, Tierney," went on Morgan, "you relieve Murphy in the morning, and watch things until I can get on the job. After I relieve yon, you get in touch with Headquarters and have some fingerprint photos taken."

"Did you find finger prints?" exclaimed Tierney, sitting up with a start.

"No," explained Morgan, "but I found the marks of the sides of somebody's hands on the dining room table in that flat. I want them prepared and photographed just as if they were fingerprints."

"But you can't identify anybody by marks of that kind," remarked Tierney, with an inquiring note in his voice.

"Probably not," Morgan returned. "I haven't the slightest idea how I could make use of such a photo now. But I want to provide against anything that may turn up. The marks are there, and we might as well have a record of them."

Tierney opened his mouth to reply, but at that instant Morgan held up a warning hand.

In many of the older and smaller apartments, such as the one occupied by Morgan, the door from the main hall opens directly into the living room. Such was the arrangement here, and Morgan slowly turned his head toward this door and listened intently. Then he carefully arose from his chair, moved softly around the corner of the table, and slowly tiptoed toward the door. Tierney had not heard a sound, yet he instantly became as alert as Morgan. He stood ready for a quick move, if necessary, while his right hand rested on the butt of the revolver in his hip pocket.

At that moment there was a quite audible sound outside the door. Morgan leaped forward and threw the door open. With the sound of the opening door both men heard somebody break into a hasty descent of the stairs. Morgan dashed through the door and down the stairs. Tierney followed close behind him. Before they reached the front door they heard the roar of an opened muffler and an accelerated engine, and by the time they reached the front steps there was nothing to be seen except the black shadow of an automobile without lights rapidly disappearing down Sheffield Avenue.

"Well, I'm damned!" growled Tierney, as the car disappeared.

Morgan said nothing, but stood thoughtfully gazing down the street.

"What do you make of it?" inquired Tierney.

"Let's go up again," suggested Morgan, without replying to the question.

Back in the living room, the men resumed their seats, and spoke in lowered voices.

"It's hard to tell what it means," Morgan at last replied. "That's the first time anything of the kind ever happened to me."

"How did you get wise?" asked Tierney.

"I heard the door move several times," Morgan explained. "At first I thought it was the wind, but the last time I heard it I was sure it had a different sound. It seemed to me that somebody had leaned against the door while trying to listen."

"By God!" exclaimed Tierney. "This is SOME case, Morgan. Are we spying on somebody, or is somebody spying on us? Marsh trails a girl; I chase up Marsh; and now I'm damned if I don't think somebody's chasing me, too."

"It begins to look like a bigger case than I thought, Tierney. An ordinary murderer usually gets out of town or lays low. Quite likely somebody is afraid we will unearth more than a murder. You run along now. I want to be alone to think things over. On your way home stop off and look up Murphy. Find out whether or not Marsh has left the house tonight. Telephone me what you find out."

"Sure thing," answered Tierney, and picking up his hat, hurried away.

Morgan sat down in his chair and began to refill his pipe. After lighting it, he settled back into his chair and meditated on the case. Reviewing in his mind the various bits of fact, information and incident which he now had at hand, he endeavored to separate or combine them according to their direct bearing upon the case.

In his earlier days Morgan had learned that a criminal case was something like a dusty roadway. Many tracks crossed and re-crossed one another, becoming just a bewildering mass to the untrained eye.

In the present instance, the situation in the Atwood apartment had queer aspects which seemed to connect it with the incident of the night before. The suspicious points were not so glaringly apparent, perhaps, as the circumstances which connected the man Marsh, but they were there just the same. While the Atwood situation attracted Morgan, he was inclined to believe that he had actually uncovered some other situation; of a criminal nature, perhaps, but not associated with his present investigations. To one unfamiliar with crime, the incident of Marsh following the girl might have seemed to form a connection, but Morgan realized that if there was anything between the Atwoods and Marsh, the latter would hardly have been secretly following Miss Atwood.

On the other hand, it was quite possible that a clever criminal, of the type he now suspected Marsh to be, having successfully accomplished one job, might have another in mind, which he thought he could execute before forced to make his final getaway. Instead of attributing this incident to a connection between the Atwoods and Marsh, Morgan figured that it weighed somewhat in the Atwoods' favor, while still further incriminating the man Marsh.

At this point in his reflections the telephone bell rang, and answering it, Morgan heard Tierney's voice.

"I've just seen Murphy," reported Tierney. "He says that Marsh came home about seven-thirty and has not been out since; unless he slipped out the back door. This doesn't seem likely as there is another man watching the rear. He don't know Marsh, but he would find out before he let anyone go. Murphy says he has seen a shadow pass the windows several times during the evening, and we are pretty sure that Marsh is the only person in that flat."

"All right," replied Morgan. They exchanged good-byes, and Morgan replaced the telephone on the tabouret.

Settling back into his chair once more, Morgan came to the conclusion that one or more of Marsh's confederates of the night before had simply been endeavoring to get information so as to warn Marsh whether or not he was suspected. Morgan knew that, as usual, he and Tierney had talked in guarded voices, so he felt confident that little, if any, of their conversation had been overheard. It was the anxiety of the person on the other side of the door to try and catch their words which had led him to lean heavily against the door and so warn Morgan of his presence. Morgan felt fairly certain that he would find Marsh at home the next day, and after that, if any reports could be conveyed to him, they would be of little use.

Piecing together, one by one, the various bits of evidence he had accumulated against Marsh, convin-ced Morgan that this was the man he wanted. The flattened bullet, the cigarette ashes, and the hand marks could not identify anyone. The cuff button, however, with its initial "M" was more direct in its accusation. It might be the principal hold on the suspect. Morgan admitted that the evidence was purely circumstantial, and that there was really nothing in it to convict a man in a court of law, but there was enough evidence to take Marsh up on suspicion, and past experience made him confident that once he had this man at Headquarters, the usual grilling would extract enough information from him to lead them to sufficient evidence of a positive nature.

There was, of course, still a doubt as to whether or not an actual crime had been committed. But something surely had happened, and Morgan began to feel that the next day would throw considerable light on what it was.

Having reached these conclusions, and a determination to visit Marsh the next day and take him into custody, Morgan went to bed.

At the first note from his alarm clock the next morning, Morgan jumped promptly out of bed. After awakening his mother so that she could get his breakfast, he hastily dressed.

Just as he was swallowing the last of his coffee there came a prolonged ring at the bell. His mother went to the door, and returned with a Western Union envelope. "My final bit of evidence!" exclaimed Morgan, as he hurriedly tore off the end of the envelope and read the cablegram within. It was brief and to the point, and read just as Morgan had anticipated it would.

Marsh unknown to me. Ames.

CHAPTER VII

MR. MARSH

Morgan had hardly expected such an early reply when he sent his inquiry to Mr. Ames regarding his acquaintance with Marsh. It was possible, however, that Mr. Ames had made an early morning call on his London bankers, and had immediately dispatched his reply. Morgan was glad that it had arrived at this opportune moment. With Murphy to testify that Marsh had claimed Ames as a friend, and with this cablegram to prove the falsity of the claim, he had at least one unanswerable piece of evidence of a suspicious nature to warrant his proposed action against the man.

Bidding his mother good-bye, Morgan hurried around to the elevated station. He purchased a package of cigarettes at the news stand, and climbed the steps two at a time to catch a train he heard approaching. A few minutes later he got off at the Wilson Avenue station, crossed Wilson Avenue to Sheridan Road, and turning north soon spotted Tierney at the corner of Lawrence Avenue.

"Hello," Morgan greeted him. "Any news?"

"No," replied Tierney. "I relieved Murphy at six o'clock this morning, and another man has taken up the watch in the alleyway. Murphy saw nothing of Marsh, and he said the light went out in his flat about 10:30. The man who watched the alleyway didn't see a soul except the milkman. Marsh came out a little while ago and I followed him. He had a quick breakfast in the waffle shop just below here, and I trailed him back again."

"I guess I'll find my man in, all right," said Morgan. "I'll go up now. You tell the man in the alleyway to keep his eyes open while I'm inside. In about ten minutes, if he doesn't hear anything from me, he can come up and wait outside Marsh's door. We'll leave him there that long in case Marsh should try to slip out the back way when he hears me at the door. If he doesn't hear from me in ten minutes he can be sure that I got in. He will then probably be more useful close at hand in the event that anything should slip up. After you tell him what to do, you can go ahead with the photographs."

Tierney nodded in acknowledgment of these instructions and started back to the alleyway. Morgan entered the apartment house, climbed the stairs to Marsh's door, and rang the bell. Marsh immediately opened the door. It seemed to Morgan as if Marsh must have been standing there awaiting his ring, yet how could the man have suspected Morgan's intention to call on him at this time? It looked strangely like the man had been on watch at the door.

"Good morning," said Marsh.

"Good morning," returned Morgan. "I want to have a little talk with you."

Marsh invited him in with a pleasant ring in his voice, and indicated the living room with a motion of his hand. Morgan entered and sat down on a chair close to the entrance, laying his hat on the floor by the chair. Marsh watched Morgan sit down in this strategical location, and then, with a slight smile, strolled across and seated himself in a big chair near the fireplace. Resting his elbows on the arms of the chair, and interlacing his fingers in front of him, he looked at Morgan.

"Well?" he said.

Morgan unbuttoned his coat and exhibited his badge. "I am Detective Sergeant Morgan of the Chicago Police Department."

"Oh, yes - Dave Morgan."

Morgan looked at Marsh sharply. "You've heard of me before, have you?" he said.

"Not until early Tuesday morning," smiled Marsh. "Then I heard one of the policemen refer to the fact that this would be a job for Dave Morgan. Evidently you have quite a reputation here in Chicago, Mr. Morgan."

"Among crooks - yes," snapped Morgan. The easy attitude of the other man was just a little puzzling. Morgan, however, was inclined to attribute it to his confidence that they were not in a position to actually fasten any guilt upon him. He suspected that the man was playing a game, and this not only nettled him, but served to strengthen his suspicions. Morgan went on.

"I have been assigned to this murder case upstairs, Mr. Marsh. After considerable investigation I find it will be necessary to ask you a few questions."

Marsh nodded but said nothing.

Morgan sat silent for a moment, as if considering how to begin. Then, without apparently looking at Marsh, he suddenly said, "It's a long jump from Mexico to Chicago."

Marsh unclasped his fingers for a moment and looked hard at Morgan. Morgan caught what he believed to be a start, but gave no indication that it had made an impression upon him.

"I was wondering," he continued, slowly, "what had brought you such a long way."

"Obviously, Mr. Morgan, if you know that much about me, you must also know that I came here on business."

"When do you attend to your business, Mr. Marsh?" asked Morgan, now looking him in the eye.

"At various times of the day," replied Marsh. "Whenever I can get appointments with the people I am negotiating with. I don't quite understand the trend of these questions, but I might say that I was downtown on business the greater part of yesterday afternoon."

"Does standing on a Michigan Avenue curb constitute the principal part of your business, Mr. Marsh?"

"Well, I sometimes fill in my time like that until I am

sure the people who are interested in my movements have gone on about their own business."

It was Morgan's turn to look disconcerted. Evidently he had a clever man to deal with, and he began to wonder if his present step had not been too precipitate. He felt sure that it was going to be difficult to fasten anything on this man. He decided, however, that he had gone too far to draw back now, and he went on with his questions.

"In the preliminary report which was given me," he said, "I noticed that you made a statement to the patrolman you called in that the noise in the flat above aroused both you and your wife."

"Yes," admitted Marsh. "I believe I did say something like that."

"But," added Morgan, "we have not been able to get an interview with your wife."

"Such an interview would be quite useless. As a matter of fact, she knows no more, and probably not so much as I do about what took place."

"You're probably right about that," smiled Morgan, and there was a sarcastic ring in his voice. "Just the same, I'd like to have a few words with her."

"You know as well as I do, Mr. Morgan, that that would be impossible."

Morgan raised his eyebrows. "I don't get you," he said.

"Well, to be more explicit, then, you know that my

wife does not live here."

"Here's a new game," thought Morgan. There was no doubt that Marsh was openly fencing with him. In fact, the man seemed to know every move which had been made. At last the super-criminal of literature seemed to have stepped into actual life. Morgan was certain that some crime had been committed, and the circumstantial evidence against this man had been accumulating rapidly. Yet, as he faced him and thought it over, he realized how intangible was their hold upon Marsh. Of course, when they got this man down to Headquarters they might force him to give more explicit details regarding his past and present actions, but a man so clever as this had probably left little behind him that would convict him of anything; certainly not of his connection with whatever had taken place in the apartment above. The cuff button, even, seemed to be growing doubtful in value.

These reflections on Morgan's part flashed through his mind so quickly that there was only the slightest pause between Marsh's last statement and the next question.

"What would give yon that impression?" asked Morgan.

"Your man went through my apartment yesterday, and I'm sure he found no evidence of a lady occupying it with me."

Morgan found it difficult to conceal his astonishment, not only at the statement, but the man's intimate knowledge of things of which he was supposed to be in ignorance. Then he remembered the clandestine listener at his door, and his doubts of a moment before took flight.

"It is quite evident," declared Morgan, "that you, or someone connected with you, have taken an unusual interest in the movements of the Chicago Police Department. Why?"

"I have taken no special interest in what you have been doing," said Marsh. "It was not difficult to note that almost from the time I called the attention of your man on the beat to the occurrence, your men have been regarding me with suspicion. I cannot possibly understand why this should be so, but you will admit that it is a fact, won't you?"

Morgan remained silent.

"I could not help noticing," continued Marsh, "that the man who had been conducting an investigation in this house was keeping watch across the street. Happening to glance back after entering a taxicab yesterday, I observed this man entering another taxi, which followed mine downtown. It was obvious to the most ordinary intelligence that he was following me. After I reached the 'loop' district I was absolutely sure of it. Then, when I returned and found footmarks in my apartment, it was quite evident that someone had been investigating."

Morgan was stunned. "Footmarks!" he thought. "Had Tierney been so clumsy and careless as to enter the flat with muddy shoes?" Something had to be done to cover an awkward pause, and give him a chance to gather his wits, so Morgan took out the package of cigarettes. After helping himself to one, he tossed the package to Marsh. Morgan noted with satisfaction that the man took one before handing the package back. Marsh smoked cigarettes!

"Why did you follow Miss Atwood?" Morgan suddenly shot at him.

Marsh's face expressed surprise. "Follow Miss Atwood!" he exclaimed.

"That's what it looked like," asserted Morgan.

"Well, that WAS a strange coincidence," commented Marsh.

Morgan found it hard to determine whether this was a reply or an evasion. He decided, however, that matters had gone far enough, and that Marsh must either prove himself innocent, or stay in jail until they could definitely fasten his guilt upon him. To bring matters to a head, he reached into his pocket for the cablegram.

"You said that Mr. Ames, the man who rents the flat upstairs, was a friend of yours."

"I believe I did," admitted Marsh.

"Well, I have a cablegram here from Mr. Ames," stated Morgan, as he brought out the paper. "Read it."

Marsh leaned forward, took the cablegram, read it gravely, and returned it to Morgan.

"You have certainly got me tied up," he said.

"Tight as a drum!" agreed Morgan. "The game's up,

Marsh. You're coming with me to Headquarters."

"I'm afraid you have sort of spilled the beans, Morgan," laughed Marsh, rising.

Morgan, however, was used to the last minute plays of cornered criminals. Leaning back in his chair, and smiling encouragingly, his hands, without seeming purpose, were slipped into the side pockets of his coat. The right hand quickly gripped a revolver in readiness.

"Yes," continued Marsh, "I had hoped to work quietly, but this incident has upset my plans. Yet, after all, perhaps we can work together with greater success."

"Now we come to the 'divvy' proposition," thought Morgan. He remained expectantly silent, however, and his face still wore its encouraging smile.

Marsh came closer and the end of the concealed revolver barrel moved upward just a trifle. The next moment the smile on Morgan's face faded out and his eyes filled with an astonished stare.

Marsh had thrown back his coat, revealing the badge of the United States Secret Service!

CHAPTER VIII

A DEFINITE CLUE

"You can take your hand off that gun now," suggested Marsh, as he smiled at Morgan and went back to his chair. "I'll tell you my part of the story, and perhaps we'll find in the end that two heads are better than one."

"You have made a big but perhaps a natural mistake. If you doubt my word in anything I am about to tell you, it will only be necessary for you to consult the Secret Service branch in the Federal Building, to confirm my status in this case."

"Without any intention of trying to kid you, Morgan, I want to say this - you've done some quick and clever work in approximately twenty-four hours. I realized from the first that things had framed themselves in a peculiar way against me. Yet, I will say frankly, that I did not expect a local policeman to put the facts together so quickly."

"I am only human, Marsh," broke in Morgan, "and your appreciation sounds good to me. But let's get down to the story."

"Quite right," agreed Marsh. "It begins two years ago.

At that time the Government discovered that counterfeit five-dollar bills were appearing in the East. They put me on the case and I traced them from city to city. Suddenly the output seemed to stop. For a time I was at loose ends, and then I had word that they were appearing again in St. Louis. I made a quick jump to that city. Counterfeit five-dollar bills are comparatively easy to pass. A larger bill may attract attention, but five dollars is a commonly used unit. For that reason few people could remember and describe the person who had tendered the bill. But to make a long story short, I finally brought their source close to a man named Atwood, by finding out that his daughter Jane occasionally paid for things with this particular series of counterfeit five-dollar notes."

"I located this man's home, where he lived with his wife and daughter. Neighbors believed him to be a traveling man as he was away a great deal. I never got a look at the man, because in some way he evidently got wind that we were watching him and stayed away from the house. From neighbors, however, I learned that he was tall, well built, dark haired and wore a small mustache. Not exactly a definite description, but one which might help in connection with other things. Finally, I got a new clue from Detroit, which seemed to indicate that I would find the man there. It came to nothing, however, and when I returned to St. Louis I found that Atwood's wife had died in the meantime - that he had stored his furniture, and his daughter was living in an hotel. I figured that there was nothing to do but keep a close watch on her from that time on, and eventually get in touch with Atwood; then, through him, locate the other members of the gang. While there was no direct evidence that such was the case, we know from experience that in a counterfeiting case there are almost always two or more persons engaged in the work."

"One night this girl gave me the slip, and it took me nearly two weeks to trace her to Chicago. Keeping watch on places where these bills occasionally appeared, I recognized her one day, and then located her in this apartment building. Now experience had shown that this case was really a game of patience. So far, little had been accomplished by hanging around the streets and watching the girl. A vacant apartment in this very building gave me an unusual opportunity."

"You know, Morgan, there are few crimes that the Government looks on with such severity as counterfeiting. To apprehend a counterfeiter they will go to any lengths and spend any amount of money. So I received permission to rent this apartment. It gave me the advantage of not only being right in the building constantly, without attracting special attention, but as I was on the floor below the suspects, I had an excellent opportunity to keep an eye on all who passed up and down the stairs. Another fortunate circumstance was the fact that the apartment over me was unoccupied. There could be no question as to where people passing up and down the stairs were going."

"Government men, as you know, Morgan, usually work with the utmost secrecy. Our own local men were not even supposed to know I was here unless the time came when I should need help. It was not logical, therefore, for me to disclose my identity or give any hint of it to the real estate firm that rented me the apartment. That was why I posed as a ranch owner from Mexico, here in Chicago for the purpose of interesting certain financial interests in my property.

That left out the entangling subject of references. Naturally, I did not want to waste money on the complete furnishing of an apartment which might be vacated at any moment, so I simply furnished up that part of it which might come under the eye of a stranger. And certainly these two rooms afforded me all the comfort that I required."

"But Marsh," interrupted Morgan. "Why did you make those breaks about your wife, and knowing Ames upstairs?"

"A man in your line of work, Morgan, ought to understand the wife idea, now that you know some of the facts. A supposedly married man passes quite unnoticed, but just give the ladies a hint that a bachelor is in the house and immediately everyone focuses attention upon him. He is a poor, lonesome man, to be pitied, and every woman in the house would have lain awake nights figuring how she could introduce me to a marriageable young woman. So I invented Mrs. Marsh as a protection."

"I'll admit that my claim of friendship with Ames didn't work out well in this instance. However, it was an idea conceived in a hurry, and in the ordinary course of events would have really attracted little, if any, attention. You realize that I was in this house to watch certain people without disclosing my identity in any way. I knew positively that the flat over me was closed and empty. Then I was awakened suddenly in the night by a most suspicious disturbance. Naturally, I connected it immediately with the people I was watching. If I took an active interest in this trouble it

might force my hand, because a moment's consideration will show you that the connection was only a
guess on my part, and MIGHT not be a fact. My first
thought, therefore, was to get the local police on the
job as quickly as possible and still keep in touch with
the incident myself."

"You may ask why I didn't telephone the Police
Department, instead of running into the street. When I
looked at my watch I saw that it was two o'clock, and I
knew from observation that a patrolman was likely to
be within a block or two of the house at that hour. On
the other hand, if I telephoned, it might be twenty
minutes before your men arrived, and you know,
Morgan, that a lot can happen in twenty minutes."

"After your man had telephoned for help he was
disinclined to have me butt into the matter any further.
Yet, you can see how imperative it was for me to be on
the job as well as your men. The first thought, and the
most logical excuse, which came to my mind, was to
tell the patrolman that the tenant of the flat was a
personal friend of mine. This made it seem perfectly
natural for me to follow up his interests in the matter.
As to keeping track of your movements, it was only
natural that I would want to keep in touch with your
progress in the case as much as possible."

"One question, Marsh," said Morgan. "How in thunder
could you see my partner's footsteps, as you said you
did, in your apartment?"

Marsh laughed.

"Through a very simple precaution that I have taken
ever since I moved in here - a little talcum powder

sprinkled over the dining room floor. "Now, Morgan, I have laid my cards on the table. You can see the close connection that probably exists between the Atwood counterfeiting case and whatever took place in the flat over us. If you have found out anything, outside of what you supposed to be my connection with the case, I would like to have the information.

"So that you can see how close the connection between the two cases really is, I will tell you that after your men left Tuesday morning, I did a little further investigating on my own account, and found what I believed to be a definite clue to the Atwoods' connection with the trouble."

"What was that?" asked Morgan.

"A SMALL SMEAR OF BLOOD ON THE DOORKNOB OF THE ATWOOD APARTMENT!"

The fact that Marsh, who had been surrounded by such suspicious circumstances that Morgan had been enabled to build up one of his quickest cases, had now turned out to be an operative of the Federal Government, was one of the most astounding things with which Morgan had ever met. It was obvious that for once in his life he had followed persistently on a blind trail, and now found himself only a little better off than when he started. Naturally, his professional pride was hurt, but the candid way in which Marsh had, to use his own words, laid his cards on the table, appealed to Morgan. He felt that this Government man was both broad-minded and efficient. He realized that there was surely more to gain by accepting Marsh's proposition, and working with him, than there would be if each worked alone, and very probably at cross purposes. The story which Marsh had told him, the surprising clue he had just offered, and the facts in his own possession, showed conclusively the close connection between the affair of the empty apartment and the Atwood counterfeiting case. Locating the murderer would undoubtedly bring the counterfeiters to light, and in the same way, locating the counterfeiters would probably disclose the perpetrator of this now unquestioned crime.

Morgan covered up these deliberations by getting out his pipe and tobacco pouch and lighting up. "Now I can talk," he said, as he leaned back in his chair.

"I may have a few facts that you don't know, Marsh, and now that I know the whole situation I can see that they will probably be of some value to you. Or in any event, of value to both of us in the general working out of the case. For I want to say that I am satisfied with your suggestion about our working together."

"I called on this Miss Atwood yesterday. While some of the information which she gave me simply ties up with and confirms your own story, there was one thing I discovered that may help us. Of course, in lining up my evidence, I separated the strong points against you from certain suspicious circumstances connected with the Atwoods. That girl impressed me so favorably that I could not definitely connect her with the trouble upstairs. Instead, I was inclined to believe that I had uncovered something else."

"During my talk with the girl I noticed a peculiar mark on her arm. I brought the conversation around to that mark, and she told me that some time during the night of the crime she had been awakened by a sharp sting in the arm, but had almost immediately gone to sleep again. Noticing the mark in the morning, she was under the impression, so she said, that it was a bite, from some kind of insect - I suggested a spider. But the truth was, Marsh, that mark was made by a hypodermic needle!"

"In my experience I have come into contact with lots of dope users. I know just how they act, talk and look - and THAT GIRL IS NOT A DOPE FIEND. In my opinion there are only two solutions to that mark on the girl's arm. Either she has not slept well of late, and decided to use something to help her, or else somebody jabbed her without her knowledge. The first explanation is hardly likely, because sleeplessness is treated in other ways. Now that you tell me this man Atwood is a criminal, and that you found a bloodstain on the doorknob, I am convinced that someone gave her an injection of morphine so that this job could be pulled without her knowledge. You probably know as well as I do, that the small purple mark, accompanied by the swelling, which I noticed on her arm, would result only from the hasty and careless use of the hypodermic needle."

"What you tell me, Morgan," said Marsh, "confirms what I have thought for some time. That is, that Jane Atwood is only the innocent tool of her father, and the gang behind him. Perhaps not even that. She exhibits none of the instincts or earmarks of the criminal woman, and no woman with easy money at her command would spend the hours and hard work which she does in the study of music. Confidentially, Morgan, I like the girl, and what I have just told you is one of the reasons why I have never attempted to arrest her and force a confession. I felt that all I could really do was to keep her under surveillance until such time as I could catch one of the real criminals getting in touch with her. The father and his gang have either simply been using her to a limited extent to pass their counterfeit notes, or else he has included a few with money which he gave her. Possibly he has maintained her in a home to have a background of respectability to which he could retire in emergencies. Letting her use counterfeit notes may have been just one of the slips of which every criminal is guilty. A really clever man is also clever enough to know that it doesn't pay to be a criminal. No matter how long the rope, there is always an end to it."

"Well," said Morgan, "there's no question that as matters now stand, that girl is our only working point. I have already called on her, and disclosed my identity as a detective, so as far as I am concerned there is little that can be done in that direction. You, as a tenant in this house, however, could cultivate her acquaintance without arousing any real suspicions on her part."

"I have been watching for an opportunity to strike up an acquaintance for a long time," replied Marsh, "but no such opportunity has as yet presented itself. You can rest assured, however, that I am ready when it does."

Just then Marsh sat up and listened, as footsteps sounded over their heads.

"That's all right, Marsh," smiled Morgan. "Those are my men taking fingerprint photographs. That was the next point I was going to tell you about - my discoveries in that apartment."

"You found fingerprints?" cried Marsh.

"No, just the marks of the sides of two hands. Apparently not of much use - but then you never can tell."

Morgan suddenly jumped to his feet. "Good Lord!" he exclaimed, "that reminds me. I forgot that I had a man sitting outside on the stairs. He'll be wondering what has happened." With that Morgan went to the door and told the plain-clothes man, who had been waiting outside, that everything was going smoothly and he could go back to the station. Returning to his chair, Morgan took up the subject of the clues he had discovered in the apartment. After recounting his discovery of the cuff button, he added, "and that was one of the most damning pieces of evidence which I had against you, Marsh - the letter - "M" on that cuff button."

"That would not have gone very far," laughed Marsh, "because I've never worn an initialed cuff button in my life. In fact, Morgan, it could have been only a clue - not evidence - for it would have been simple, when the loss was discovered, to also lose the duplicate. That cuff button may or may not be a clue. Of course, the tenant's initials do not coincide with the initial on that button, but it might have been dropped by a servant or a friend. As a matter of fact, that button might have been lying under the cabinet for sometime before Ames went to Europe. However, it's something worth having and remembering, for one never can tell when even a little thing like that may give some lead that would prove worth while."

"How would you analyze that flattened bullet?" asked Morgan.

"The shot was fired at close range," Marsh replied. "It may have passed clear through the person fired at. That bullet is worth remembering, however, just like the cuff button. Some day it may fit in with and explain other evidence."

"There is one more point," added Morgan, "that may or may not have a bearing on this case. Last night, while my partner Tierney and. myself were conferring on this case at my house, somebody tried to listen outside my door. I was pretty sure this was so from the sounds I heard; and when I went to the door, somebody dashed down the stairs and escaped in a motor car. I'm ashamed to say it, now, but at the time I suspected it was one of your confederates."

"You've been mixed up in a good many cases, Morgan, and probably have some half-finished affairs in the back of your head right now. I would say that such an occurrence could be connected with any one of these. On the other hand, this case is very fresh, and you have been active in working it up. Some person may be trying to find out just how close you are getting to the trail, so as to take precautions, if necessary."

At that moment there was a scream in the hall outside Marsh's door. Both men sprang to their feet and Marsh leaped to the door.

CHAPTER IX

THE LAST LETTER

At the same moment that Marsh opened the door, Tierney and the man from Headquarters, who had been taking the photographs, came bounding down the stairs from the third floor.

They all saw the body of a woman lying motionless on the landing.

"Who is it?" cried Morgan, over Marsh's shoulder.

"Jane Atwood!" was the sharp reply.

With that Marsh stooped and took the unconscious girl up in his arms, the unusual tenderness and care of his movements being plainly apparent. Carrying her into his apartment, while the others followed, Marsh laid her gently on a davenport in the living room.

"She must have had a shock of some kind and fainted," exclaimed Morgan.

"No," returned Marsh, as he softly smoothed back the hair from her forehead, disclosing a bruise that was now rapidly discoloring and swelling. "Somebody knocked her insensible." Then added, "You sent your man away too soon, Morgan."

"My God!" burst out Morgan. "What nerve! To think of pulling anything like this in a house full of detectives."

"We have a tough customer this time," declared Marsh. "Ordinary methods won't go. Watch her while I get some water."

Marsh went to the bathroom for a towel and some cold water. In the meantime Morgan turned sharply to Tierney.

"From now on, while we work on this case, your job is to stand outside of every door I enter."

Tierney grinned. To some men it might have seemed that they were being thrust into the background. To Tierney, however, the work immediately presented possibilities that stirred his fighting Irish blood. Without a word he went out into the public hall and closed the door behind him.

Marsh returned, and began to bathe the girl's forehead and the bruise with the cold water. While he worked over her, the photographer approached Morgan and held out an envelope.

"After your friend here picked the girl up," he explained, "I noticed this lying near her."

Morgan took the envelope. After a hasty glance he extended it to Marsh. "A letter to this girl with a St. Louis postmark!" he gasped.

"Good!" exclaimed Marsh, without stopping his work to revive the girl. "Just what I have been watching for. Open it."

Morgan understood. Turning to the photographer, he handed back the envelope. "Slip into the kitchen, steam this open and make a quick copy." Then, noticing the case on the floor beside the man, he added, "Finished your work upstairs?"

The man nodded.

"Then make a photograph of this letter at the same time. The handwriting may prove useful."

Taking the letter and picking up his case, the man went back to the kitchen. Morgan turned to Marsh.

"How is she coming on?" he inquired.

There was a slight flutter of the eyelids as he spoke and Marsh called his attention to it. "She will be all right in a moment," he said.

Presently Jane Atwood's eyes opened slowly, and she gazed in a bewildered and uncomprehending way at the two men bending anxiously over her. Marsh continued to bathe her forehead and gradually she seemed to realize her position. She struggled slowly into a sitting position on the davenport while the two men stood back, awaiting her first words. Contrary to the usual idea of feminine return to consciousness, she did not inquire where she was. Instead she startled the two men by asking, "Did you get him?"

"Get who?" counter questioned Marsh, taking the lead.

"The man who was outside the door," was the reply.

Marsh and Morgan exchanged quick glances. To them it was a confirmation that the listener of the night before was still seeking information about the case in hand. Moreover, here might be a clue to his identity, or at least a description that would prove helpful, so Marsh seated himself on the davenport at her side, while Morgan went to a chair across the room.

Both men knew instinctively that this would put the girl more at her ease than if they continued to stand over her like inquisitors. Marsh continued the conversation. "We know nothing about what happened," he said. "We heard a scream. When we opened the door you were lying there. No one was around except two policemen who came down from the third floor at that moment, having also heard your cry."

After this simple statement of the situation, Marsh paused, waiting for the girl to go on. He felt that in her dazed and weakened condition questions would still further bewilder her, might even cause a revulsion that would delay or prevent their getting information that would prove of inestimable value.

The girl paused, as if to collect her thoughts, and passed her hand before her eyes with a motion similar to sweeping aside a curtain. Then she spoke.

"I went to the hairdresser's in the block below. Returning, I stopped to take a letter out of the mail box and then started up the stairs to my apartment." At this point she passed her hand over her hair and smiled as she realized its disheveled appearance now. "As I turned up the flight to this floor, I saw a man crouched down before the door of this apartment. He did not hear me until I reached the top of the stairs. Then he jumped up, and seeing me, tried to push by. Remembering the burglary, or whatever it was, upstairs, I knew I should try to stop him. So I seized his coat and we started to struggle. Instantly I saw him draw back his arm, then I felt the blow. I remember nothing of what happened from that moment until I awoke just now on this davenport."

Marsh sat up and clenched his hands. "If I knew what the fellow looked like I would thrash him the next time I saw him," he threatened, hoping thus to draw out the description he wanted.

"Oh, I can describe him - at least in a general way. He was short, not much over five feet, and quite thin. His face had a peaked look. While we struggled his hat fell off and I saw that he was almost bald. His nose was large, and taken with his thin face and rather large bright eyes, it seems to me now that he looked just like an eagle."

"Had you ever seen him before?" Morgan asked.

"Never," she answered, and the positive note in her voice could not be mistaken.

"I will send your description to all the stations," said Morgan. "We will try to get that fellow."

Morgan went to the telephone and called the Detective Bureau. He gave the necessary directions, and as he returned to his chair, remarked, "In an hour or two this won't be a safe town for that fellow."

"You are the detective who came to see me!" exclaimed the girl. "Perhaps this is the man you are looking for."

"Perhaps," agreed Morgan. "I can tell better after I get my hands on him."

"Oh, my!" cried the girl, and began to search about the davenport.

The two men suspected she was looking for the letter, and they were relieved to see the photographer appear in the doorway at that moment.

"Have yon lost something?" inquired Marsh.

"Yes, the letter I took out of the mail box."

"Here it is, Miss," said the photographer, stepping forward and presenting the letter to her. "I picked it up in the hall where you dropped it."

She took it and thanked him. "I'm so glad you found it," she added. "It is from my father, and I have not heard from him in a long time. I feel better now and will go home."

She rose slowly with the words. Noting her weakness, Marsh stepped to her side and slipped his arm under hers.

"Let me help you up the stairs," he said, gently.

"Thank you," she returned, simply, realizing her need of help.

"I'll wait until you come back, Marsh," said Morgan.

The girl started. "Are you Mr. Marsh?" she exclaimed. Then, as Marsh nodded, she added, "Why, you are the man who sent this detective up to see me."

Marsh glanced quickly at Morgan, who, behind the girl's back, dropped one eyelid slowly and significantly.

"Well, you seemed the most likely person to have information, being right on the same floor," Marsh said, smiling.

There could be no question that this was a natural explanation, and the girl seemed satisfied. With a nod and a smile to Morgan and the photographer, she allowed Marsh to assist her out of the door and up the stairs to her apartment. Tierney rose from the step where he had been sitting, to let her pass, and she favored him with one of her pretty smiles as he did so. Tierney then climbed after them to the next landing and stood watching. Marsh waited until the door closed after her. Then, with a catch in his breath that sounded suspiciously like a sigh, he went back to his apartment. Tierney gave him a peculiar look as he passed.

The photographer had gone, but Morgan held out the copy which he had made of the letter as soon as Marsh entered, with the remark, "Now, what's the game?"

Marsh took it and read:

My dear Daughter:

I have returned from the last trip I shall ever make. I

have never told you, not wishing to cause you worry, but my health has been gradually failing for many years.

I can no longer attend to my duties on the road and have had to give up my position. The doctor gives me but a few months to live, so rather than be a burden to you I have decided to end the thing at once. When this letter reaches you, the Mississippi will be carrying my body to the sea, where I hope that it will be lost to the world forever.

Knowing that my time was approaching, I long ago arranged for your future. If you will identify yourself to the National Trust Company, Chicago, you will find that you have been amply provided for. As we do not lease the apartment direct from the owner, you had better move out at once and go to an hotel. No one can hold you responsible.

Good luck and success in your music. God bless you, and good-bye.

Your devoted father.

"What's the game?" repeated Morgan, when he saw that Marsh had finished reading the letter.

"A convenient disappearance, that is all," returned Marsh. "Things were beginning to get too hot for him. No doubt he thought you were getting closer than you really were. Poor girl," he added. "She will take it as gospel truth, and we dare not tell her otherwise - not now, anyway."

"One thing is certain in my mind now," asserted Morgan. "There was a murder upstairs. They planned to put some person who was becoming a menace, quietly out of the way. But you spoiled it!"

"No, I did not spoil it," said Marsh. "The shot did that. I have felt for some time that that shot was a mistake - a slipup somewhere."

"I've got to go; it is two o'clock," exclaimed Morgan as he looked at his watch. "Where shall we hold future conferences! I do not want to be seen coming here too often. It might lead to suspicions of you, and I think we can accomplish more if your connection with the case is not made clear."

"How about your house?" inquired Marsh. "Knowing that you are now suspicious, and with Tierney on the doorstep, they will probably keep away from there in the future."

"Well, let it stand at that for the present," agreed Morgan. "Telephone me when you want to come. My number is in the telephone book."

With that the two men's hands met in a strong grip as if to seal their future partnership. Morgan opened the door and then started back with a cry.

Tierney lay stretched out across the landing, apparently asleep.

But Morgan knew the man better.

CHAPTER X

THE STOLEN SUITCASE

The placing of Tierney on guard in the hall had been an impulsive act on Morgan's part. It was more to put an idea into immediate execution than to actually have a protecting outpost at this time, for the very nature of his experience would have told Morgan that after the mysterious attack upon Jane Atwood there would be little possibility of a similar occurrence the same day. The instant he saw Tierney lying in the hall, however, he realized that the man had been the victim of a somewhat similar attack, and the mere thought that such a thing was possible stunned him into inaction for a moment. The next minute both he and Marsh were kneeling at Tierney's side and endeavoring to arouse him.

Morgan removed Tierney's cap and passed his hand around over the man's head until he found a slight lump, a little back of the right ear.

"Knocked out with a black-jack!" he cried. "How could a man get that close to Tierney without being heard!"

"The carpet in these halls and on the stairs is well padded," explained Marsh. "I have noticed on a number of occasions that people passing up and down these stairs make very little noise unless a foot happens to strike the woodwork. And you can be sure of one thing, Morgan, this man must have been pretty close at hand. He got into action without having to do much climbing."

"Or descending," added Morgan, suddenly, looking at Marsh.

"If he came DOWN the stairs, Morgan, then the girl has certainly been pulling the wool over our eyes."

Morgan shook his head doubtfully. "Well, I'll acknowledge that it takes a pretty wise detective to understand a woman."

At this moment, Tierney showed signs of coming back to life. His eyes opened and looked at them with a dazed stare. Almost instantly this changed to a savage glare. His two arms shot up, seized the men leaning over him and pulled them down. Like most people who have been knocked. unconscious, Tierney had no idea of the intervening lapse of time. Before becoming unconscious he had probably realized that he was attacked, and he was now taking up the fight where he had left off.

"Hold on, Tierney - this is Morgan - Morgan - do you understand? And this is Marsh with me!"

The two men held Tierney down until he had a chance to collect his thoughts. Then he smiled sheepishly as he looked from one to the other. "What the - !" he began; then paused.

They jerked him to his feet and set him down on the

stair. There he sat for a moment, rubbing the sore spot on his head, of which he now began to be conscious.

"Guess I'd better resign," he said, dolefully, coming to a full realization of the situation. "A detective ain't much use after he begins to need a bodyguard."

"Cut the nonsense, Tierney," admonished Morgan. "Tell us what happened."

"That's what I'd like to know," growled Tierney.

"Well then," suggested Morgan, "tell us what happened up to the point where you don't know anything."

"Let's see," reflected Tierney. "When you sent me out into the hall, the first thing I did was to go part way up this flight of stairs and make sure that all was clear above. Then I sat down exactly where I am sitting now, but close to the stair rail. I figured that if anybody came up the stairs I could see him before he spotted me. I heard a couple of people go out downstairs, but everything was quiet up here. I kept my eye on your friend here while he took the girl upstairs. After he went in I settled back in the same place again. Finally I felt like a smoke. There didn't seem much chance of anybody coming back again, so I figured I might as well have a smoke and I got out my pipe. While I was lighting up, something hit me. You know the rest better than I do."

"But," expostulated Morgan, "you're no green hand, Tierney. How could anybody sneak up behind you without your hearing them?"

Tierney looked foolish for a moment, then brightened

up. "Morgan," he said, "I've got the dope. That old pipe of mine was wheezing like a sick horse when I began to pall on it. That's what gave the fellow his chance. I'll admit it, Morgan - I should have known better than to light it in the first place."

"All right, Tierney, you've learned your lesson. But I'm afraid you let something good slip by you."

"It is my opinion," Marsh broke in, "that he has let the most important actor in the drama get away. The man must have been pretty desperate to take such a chance, and I doubt if anyone but the leading character would have been so anxious to get away quickly and unseen. Now then, let us go up to the Atwood apartment. I will assume the role of protector to Miss Atwood while you two, whom she knows to be detectives, can search the flat."

At this, Tierney stood up on the stairs and looked suspiciously at Marsh. Then, as Morgan agreed to the idea, Tierney turned toward him and exclaimed, "Say, you gone crazy?"

Morgan gazed at him in astonishment.

Marsh laughed. "Tierney is still suspicious," he said.

Morgan's face lit up with understanding. Going over to Tierney, he whispered in his ear,

"Well, I'm damned!" Tierney mumbled.

The three men then climbed the stairs to the Atwood apartment, and Morgan's hand was already on the push button of the electric bell when there was an exclamation from Marsh.

"Stop!" he cried. "Look here."

They instantly saw what he meant. The wood door was standing open about two inches, and there was sufficient light in the entrance hall of the apartment to show that at least no one was looking out.

"Remember, I'm in the background on this," Marsh whispered to Morgan. "You two take, the lead - but be cautious."

Morgan pulled out his revolver and Tierney followed his example. Then Morgan gave the door a quick push and stood back. It swung back against the wall with a resounding thud, but outside of that sound everything remained silent. The three men then moved warily into the doorway, with Tierney and Morgan in the lead. While Marsh remained in the entrance hall, Tierney stepped into the living room and Morgan crept cautiously through the portieres into the dining room. So silently did these two men move that Marsh heard, nothing until, a moment later, he saw Morgan step back through the portieres. The doors of both the bedroom and the bathroom stood open and Morgan, without saying anything to Marsh, investigated these two rooms. Then he returned to the entrance hall and spoke to Marsh, who had already been joined by Tierney.

"Not a soul in the flat but the girl," whispered Morgan. "She's in a chair in the dining room, and apparently unconscious again. There's an odor of chloroform in the dining room!"

Marsh sprang through the dining room portieres, followed by the others. He found Jane Atwood in a rocking chair near one of the windows. She was apparently unconscious, but there were convulsive movements of her body. Marsh sniffed the aromatic odor and nodded. "I don't think they gave her much," he said. "She's just barely unconscious. I'll try to revive her while you two look things over more carefully."

Morgan turned to Tierney. "You take another look at the front," he directed. "Look through all the drawers and closets, but be careful not to leave anything upset."

Tierney promptly started on his work of investigation. Morgan turned back into the kitchen. He had previously noticed that the maid's room was upset and he wanted to examine this room again. The bed was made up, but as the linen was fresh and unwrinkled it seemed certain that no one had occupied it recently. The chief cause of the disorder seemed to have been a hasty examination of the closet. A roll of blankets and some other articles that had evidently been on the shelf of the closet had been pulled down and scattered over the bedroom floor. A couple of suits, and other articles of men's attire, were hung on the hooks, apparently undisturbed. Morgan saw that a speedy search had been made for something. Whether or not the object had been found it was impossible to say.

Going back into the kitchen, and trying the rear door, he discovered that, though closed, it was unlocked. He locked it, and returning to the dining room, found that Marsh had succeeded in reviving the girl. Tierney was also there, and the two men were chatting with her.

"You seem to be having a good deal of trouble today,"

said Morgan, as he neared her.

She smiled wanly at him.

"I can't understand it at all. Burglars must be extremely bold in Chicago."

"Do you think it was a burglar?" asked Morgan.

"What else could it be?" she returned. "I am sure that I have no enemies anywhere, and I haven't even any friends in Chicago."

"Are you keeping anything of special value in the house?" inquired Morgan.

"Only what you can see about you," she replied "And these rings, which have not been touched."

"You are sure you didn't have anything of value concealed in the maid's room?"

"No, that's the room my father uses when he comes home from his trips."

"Well, perhaps he had something of value there."

"I'm quite sure he did not," she said, positively.

"How do you feel now, Miss Atwood?" asked Marsh, catching the drift of the questioning.

"Just a little bewildered," she replied, "and slightly nauseated, but I think I shall be all right presently."

"Do you feel equal to looking over that room now?"

Marsh inquired.

"I think so," she said, and with Marsh's assistance, she arose from her chair.

Morgan led the way and the girl, leaning on Marsh's arm, followed.

"You see," said Morgan, when they had reached the maid's room, "somebody has pulled everything off the shelf. Is there anything missing as far as you know?"

Miss Atwood looked over the articles on the floor, glanced at the empty shelf, and at the bottom of the closet. Then she turned to Morgan. "My father had a suitcase on that shelf," she said. "I do not see it there now."

"Oh," murmured Morgan. "Was it an empty suitcase?"

"I really couldn't tell you. I never examined it, as it was always pretty well hidden under a lot of other things."

"I see," said Morgan. "The burglar evidently stole only the suitcase, thinking perhaps there was something of value in it. We'd better go now," he added, turning to the others. "Miss Atwood will want to lie down and rest after her exciting day."

When they reached the front door, Morgan turned to her. "Do you expect your father home soon, Miss Atwood?" he inquired.

"Oh," she exclaimed, "I haven't read my letter yet. You see, I had just reached the dining room when that burglar attacked me."

"You need not worry about any further disturbances or attacks, Miss Atwood," Morgan assured her. "There will be a policeman at the front and back of this house inside of an hour, and they will stay here until we clear up this case."

"And remember that I live close at hand, on the floor below, Miss Atwood," reminded Marsh. "If there is anything I can do to help you at any time, don't fail to call upon me."

"Thank you," she replied, and closed the door as the men went down the stairs.

CHAPTER XI

THE TRAIL GROWS CLEARER

"I want to use your telephone for a minute," Morgan said to Marsh, as they went down the stairs. "I want to have men put on duty here as soon as possible, and I think it would be well to send out that description you have of Atwood. We might catch him at one of the railway stations, trying to leave the city."

Marsh unlocked the door of his apartment and Morgan immediately went to the telephone. He gave the Detective Bureau a description of Atwood, added that the man would probably be carrying a suitcase, and suggested that all outgoing trains be watched. Then he got the captain of the precinct on the telephone, and after explaining the attacks that had taken place, was assured that two men would be placed on duty to watch the house within a few minutes.

"Good Lord, I'm starving to death!" cried Tierney, as Morgan left the telephone. "What time is it, anyway?"

Morgan glanced at his watch.

"Three-thirty," he replied. "Now you speak of it, Tierney, I feel kind of hungry, myself. How about you, Marsh?"

"It was on my mind to suggest a little luncheon," returned Marsh. "Suppose we run down to Sally's Waffle Shop. It's only a block south, and it would be a quiet place to talk things over while we are eating. It is a good place to eat, too. I've had nearly all of my meals there since I took this apartment."

The others agreeing, the three men then walked down to the little restaurant. As it was an off hour they were able to get a table in a secluded corner where their conversation could not be overheard.

"I think this lunch should be on me," said Morgan, as he looked at Marsh with a twinkle in his eye.

"No," objected Marsh, "I should hardly call you a loser. Your work has really disclosed a lot."

"Anyway, Headquarters will think you're doing something, Morgan," broke in Tierney. "All those descriptions you shot over the 'phone today looked as if you were getting the dope on somebody."

"I suggest," said Marsh, "that as you fellows have been my guests most of the day, you now be my guests for luncheon. Order what you like. You can get anything here from waffles to a full meal."

"A big, fat, juicy steak for mine!" cried. Tierney.

"Yes, you're an invalid, aren't you!" scoffed Morgan.

Tierney rubbed the bump on his head and grinned.

They gave their orders to the waitress, and while waiting, Morgan explained Marsh's participation in the work in reply to an anxious reminder from Tierney. The startling shattering of the net, which they believed they had drawn around Marsh, for once stunned Tierney into silence. When their hunger had been partly satisfied, Morgan reminded Marsh that they had not yet analysed the peculiar situation discovered in the Atwood apartment.

"I hurried you fellows out so we could tall over that suitcase," Morgan explained. "Of course, I've got some ideas of my own, but I'd like to know what you think, Marsh."

"Well," replied Marsh, "if you and Tierney will tell me exactly what you discovered, I'll tell you what I think."

"My part's easy to tell," said Tierney. "I didn't find anything suspicious. I spent most of the time turning over a lot of pink silk and lace things that almost made me blush. There were no letters or photographs, and as far as I could see, none of the things had been disturbed until I turned them over myself."

"And I," said Morgan, "found the mess that you saw in the maid's room. I also discovered that the back door was unlocked."

"I had a theory," explained, Marsh, "and what you say about the back door clinches it. Now, suppose you were a crook, and had committed a crime that, through careless management, had brought the police right next door to your headquarters; the place you had hoped to reserve for emergencies, as a matter of fact. Suppose you had reason to believe that they would begin to suspect you. You have long had a plan ready to throw the police off the scent, if anything should ever happen, by pretending to make away with yourself. You put the first step of this plan into execution by sending a letter stating that you are now as good as dead. Then you suddenly remember that at your refuge you have left some important evidence; something that, if discovered, might offset your well-laid plans. What would you do? You'd try to get that evidence, wouldn't you?"

"That is precisely what happened. Atwood, accompanied by one of his men, who was to stand guard, returned to his apartment to secure that almost forgotten evidence. Now, the man he left on guard heard some familiar voices, or perhaps a name he recognized. He overlooked his duty for the moment and tried to listen. He was discovered. Naturally, his first thought was of himself, and he made his escape. Up in his apartment, Atwood, who had secured what he sought, is ready to go, but is delayed by this disturbance in the hall. He doesn't know exactly, what it is, so he sticks close. Then he thinks of making his escape down the back stairs, but unfortunately some of his feminine neighbors are gossiping on the stairs below. He could not go down that way without attracting attention that might prove awkward later. Suddenly he hears the door of his apartment open, and some person enter. He watches, and discovers that his daughter has come home, alone. Now, if she should see him, his well-laid plan is ruined. Its greatest success lies in her honest conviction that he is really dead. He is trapped; front, rear and on the premises. He is desperate. Something must be done quickly. In a favorable moment he springs upon the girl from behind and renders her unconscious with chloroform. He finds the back stairs still closed to him, and in his haste forgets to lock the door as he closes it. He finds a man keeping guard on the front stairs. He decides quickly that he can deal better with this man than the women of the back. He watches and waits, leaving the door open for a quick retreat. His opportunity comes when this man's attention is directed to the lighting of a pipe. In a flash he is down the stairs, knocks the man unconscious, and goes out the front door. The next minute he is lost in the crowds on the street and is free."

"That, gentlemen, is my explanation of what happened in the house today. Of course, it is largely theory, but I believe it fits the case uncommonly well."

"I'll say you're there!" cried Tierney.

"Yes," Morgan agreed. "You talk as if you had been a spectator of the whole occurrence. I doubt if a clearer explanation could be made, and I think you came pretty near the truth when you said a little while ago that we actually had uncovered something today. There is still a mystery of some kind, but thanks to you, we are now in a position to take some definite steps toward solving it."

"Still, there is one illogical point in your surmise. The letter from St. Louis arrived sometime this morning. If Atwood was in Chicago Tuesday morning, how did he get that letter off, so quickly?"

"The trouble with an analysis based chiefly on speculation, Morgan, is that many points may seem illogical and unexplained. We can only rely definitely upon the outstanding features. However, I never adopt any explanation unless it has a basis in possibility. You remember that a while ago I told you I thought that shot was a mistake - that it was never intended a shot should be fired. Whoever was engaged in that occurrence knew that the shot would lead to a police investigation, and once the police start, there is no telling where the matter may end. To head them off quickly, is it not possible that someone left immediately for St. Louis to post that letter?"

Morgan nodded. "It's straining a point, but it's quite possible, Marsh. At least, we have no better explanation."

They had finished their meal, and after Marsh settled the bill, parted on the sidewalk; Marsh to return to his apartment and await developments there, while Morgan and Tierney undertook some investigations which Morgan had in mind.

On his return to the house, Marsh noted with satisfaction that a policeman in uniform way already on duty. However, he wanted to make sure that the girl was all right, so instead of going directly to his apartment, he continued on up the stairs to the Atwood apartment and rang the bell. After a slight pause, Miss Atwood opened the door. Her eyes were red with weeping, and she held her handkerchief so as to partly conceal her face.

"I called to see if everything was all right," explained Marsh. "Why, what has happened?"

He knew perfectly well the cause of the girl's trouble, and he had to struggle hard to assume an air of ignorance. It tore his heart to see this girl, for whom he felt a growing affection, in such distress, knowing that all the time he possessed the knowledge to sweep away her grief. And yet would it? Was it not probable that a girl like her would feel even greater grief at the knowledge that her father was a hunted criminal instead of merely dead? She presented a most pitiable figure standing there, absolutely alone in the world. She had gone through experiences that day which would have made the average woman collapse, and to cap it all she had received the final blow in the news of her father's death.

Marsh's heart went out to her: He longed to take her into his arms and ask her to allow him to henceforward be her protector. It was hard to hold himself in check, yet he knew that it was no time for this disclosure of his own feelings. Instead, he stepped quietly through the door and sat down in the living room, where the girl joined him. She wept silently for a few moments, while Marsh sat and waited. At last she spoke.

"My father is dead, Mr. Marsh."

"What a shock!" he exclaimed. "I am so sorry. How did it happen?"

"You know I received a letter from him this morning. It said that his health had failed, that he could no longer work, and that by the time the letter reached me he world have committed suicide."

Marsh's life had been devoted to running down criminals. He had had very little to do with women except those of the criminal type. He was at a loss, therefore, for words to comfort this delicate girl. He was further embarrassed by the knowledge of facts which he dared not divulge. Everything he said sounded crude and rough in his ears, but somehow his words seemed to have a soothing effect on the girl and eventually her weeping ceased.

"She's a wonder!" thought Marsh. "The bravest little woman I ever knew." Then addressing her, he said, "Miss Atwood, after all that has happened, it is not possible for you to stay here alone tonight. You should go to an hotel, where you will feel protected and secure, and at least know that, even though they are not your friends, you have people all about you." He hesitated a moment, then added, "I hope you will receive my offer in the spirit in which it is intended. If you are in any way financially embarrassed at the moment, I would be glad to take care of your hotel expenses until you can straighten out your affairs."

"hank you, Mr. Marsh," she returned. "I appreciate both your offer and the spirit in which you make it, but I am well provided with funds. Father was always generous with me, and even in his last letter he said that he had left me well provided for."

"Then pack up a bag at once, Miss Atwood, and let me escort you to some hotel. I suggest the Monmouth. It is only a couple of blocks away and I know it to be a nice, quiet family hotel where the people would be congenial. In this time of trouble you would find it a comfort to have a few women friends. I think you have made a mistake in devoting so much time to your musical studies, while neglecting social opportunities."

The girl considered a moment, then, springing up, said, "I will follow your suggestion. It would be dreadful to stay here alone tonight. In fact, now that I have no one to make a home for, it would probably be better for me to stay permanently at an hotel."

She went to her room and prepared to leave the house. She soon reappeared with a bag, which Marsh took from her. A few minutes later they parted at the desk of the Monmouth Hotel, and Marsh returned to his apartment.

It was strange how lonely the place seemed, 'now that he knew the girl was no longer under the same roof with him.

CHAPTER XII

MISSING

Two days had passed without any word from Morgan, and Marsh himself had made little progress on the case, for a large part of those two days had been taken up in assisting Jane Atwood to pack her personal things and remove them to her new home in the hotel.

They had been pleasant days for Marsh, because he had derived considerable happiness from the little services he had been able to render the girl, and also because it was the first time in all the months he had been watching over her that he was actually in her company.

During this time Marsh had made one discovery of a peculiar nature, but its working out appeared to have no particular effect on the developments of the case. The morning after he escorted Jane Atwood to the hotel, she had returned to the apartment to begin her packing. While assisting in this, Marsh had suggested that she notify the man from whom her father had rented the apartment, so that he could take steps to secure another tenant. He was amazed to learn that she knew nothing whatever about the matter, not even the name of the man from whom they rented. So during the morning, Marsh called at the office of the agent of the building and explained the situation. The agent was surprised, saying that he had always supposed a Mr. Crocker, whose name appeared on the lease, occupied the apartment himself. The man's name not appearing in the telephone directory, the agent had suggested that he would write to the man's former St. Louis address. Marsh thought this a good idea, and owing to the odd situation which had developed, left his telephone number, suggesting that the agent let him know what he heard in the matter.

The next afternoon, the real estate agent telephoned him that a telegram had just arrived from the man in St. Louis, stating that he had never rented any such apartment in Chicago, had never signed any lease, and did not know anything about the matter. To Marsh, the situation was obvious. In renting the apartment Atwood had used the name of a well known St. Louis man so as to have good references and close the deal quietly without in any way bringing his own name and personality into the matter. There was nothing in this information to help the case in any way, yet it created a strange situation. Here was an apartment full of furniture that rightfully belonged to the girl, and yet he could in no way convince her of that fact without also disclosing the other circumstances connected with the case. All that they could do was to walk out and close the door behind them, leaving the problem to the real estate agent to solve. This they did on Friday afternoon, and so far as Marsh was concerned, the Atwood apartment was of no further interest, for it was obvious, now that Atwood was supposed to be dead, no one connected with him would be likely to ever again visit the apartment. He decided, however, to remain in his own apartment for the present. The lease he had signed had still nearly a year to run. He was comfortable, and free to come and go as he pleased, without anyone noticing his movements. Then there was no telling how long he would have to remain in Chicago, for he felt that the solution of this case still rested somewhere within the city limits. At the present moment he was facing a blank wall, but any day or hour might furnish a new clue that would set things moving again. In fact, he was inclined to feel that when he again heard from Morgan, the detective would probably have valuable information for him.

It was Saturday morning, and Marsh, on his way back from breakfast at the little waffle shop, purchased a copy of the Tribune and went back to his apartment to look over the day's news. No sooner had he opened the paper than this headline met his eyes:

PROMINENT BROKER MISSING

Marsh dropped the paper on his knees and thought for a moment. Ever since Tuesday morning, when the trouble had occurred, he had carefully scanned the papers for reports of any missing people who might in any way be connected with this occurrence. Here at last was an announcement that looked promising. He began to read the article.

Richard Townsend Merton, the well known La Salle Street broker, has been missing far ten days, it was learned yesterday. Gilbert Hunt, the general manager of the Merton business, notified the police that Mr. Merton had not appeared at his office, his clubs, or his hotel for some days. A telegraphed inquiry to his wife, who resides with an invalid son in Arizona, brought the reply that Mr. Merton had not been there. The manager is inclined to believe that Mr. Merton has either wandered away during a lapse of memory, or may have met with an accident.

The article then continued with the usual outline of what the police were doing, and a description of the broker's life and habits. Marsh learned from this that Merton had closed his country home in Hubbard Woods when his wife moved to Arizona with their son. He had lived for the past two years at a downtown hotel, and spent most of his evenings at his clubs.

After reading the entire article carefully, Marsh cut out the accompanying photographs of Merton and the abset wife and son. Here was something worth investigating, he thought, for he remembered the cuff button with the initial "M," which Morgan had discovered.

For upwards of an hour Marsh sat in deep deliberation, figuring how he could get in close touch with the situation without in any way disclosing his official connection or real interest in the matter. At last he decided to follow a plan which he had used successfully in connection with two previous cases. He looked up the address of the Merton offices, and putting on his coat and hat, took the Sheridan Road motor bus downtown.

Marsh located the Merton offices on the fifteenth floor of the La Salle Trust Building, and paused a moment inside the door to look the place over. He found himself in a large room which contained several stenographers and clerks. To his left was a grill work with a window marked, "Cashier," and beyond this, several men who were evidently bookkeepers. In front of him was a railing, behind which sat a girl at a telephone switchboard. At the other side of the room, floors opened into what were evidently three private offices. On the first door he saw the name, Mr. Merton; on the second, Mr. Hunt. The third door was blank.

Approaching the girl, Marsh inquired if Mr. Hunt was in.

"Yes," she replied, looking him over. "Have you a card?"

Marsh handed her a card and she went into Mr. Hunt's office. In a moment she returned and said, "Please step in."

Marsh entered Hunt's office and closed the door behind him. It was the usual private office, with a large flat top desk in the center. This was so arranged that Hunt's back was to the light, which fell full upon any visitor's face. Some files, a bookcase, and a small table littered with papers, stood against the wall. Hunt motioned to a chair and said, "Sit down, please." Marsh's card lay before him on the desk. He picked it up and read:

GORDON MARSH
Private Investigator

Then looking at Marsh as he laid the card down, he said, "what can I do for you?"

"As you see by my card," replied Marsh, "my business consists of conducting special private investigations. I read in the morning paper that Mr. Merton is missing, and I came in to see if you would care to use my services."

"I have placed the entire matter in the hands of the police," returned Hunt.

"You probably know, as well as I do, Mr. Hunt, that that is the next thing to burying the matter. They will be very busy for a couple of days and then forget it."

"That is about what I thought, Mr. Marsh," admitted Hunt.

"But isn't it important, for business reasons, that you ascertain definitely, and as quickly as possible, just what has happened to Mr. Merton?" Marsh asked.

"To a certain extent, yes. But Mr. Merton has left the business entirely in my hands for some time, and things will continue satisfactorily in his absence."

"Then I presume you wouldn't care to have me conduct a private investigation on your behalf, Mr. Hunt?"

"Well, I'll tell you, Mr. Marsh," said Hunt. "Until you presented your card to me this morning, the thought of doing anything beside notifying the police had not occurred to me. Let me think for a minute."

With that, Hunt swung his chair around so that his back was toward Marsh, and gazed thoughtfully out of the window for a few minutes.

"In your work," he said at length, swinging around toward Marsh once more, "you probably come into more or less close contact with the police. I mean by that, that you would work with them more or less on a case of this kind."

"Certainly," replied Marsh. "I follow up every likely clue, including everything which may be unearthed by the police."

"After thinking it over, it may be that we can come to some arrangement, Mr. Marsh," said Hunt. "What are your terms?"

"My charges are $25.00 a day, and expenses," said Marsh.

"Whew!" whistled Hunt, "that's pretty steep. I could hire all the private detectives I wanted for ten dollars a day."

"But I'm not a regular detective," protested Marsh. "I'm an investigator."

"You make a distinction, do you?" smiled Hunt.

"Absolutely," asserted Marsh. "I merely dig up the facts and turn them over to you for any action you see fit. My investigative work could hardly be classed with the ordinary work of the detective."

Hunt clasped his hands before him on the desk. After a moment's thought, he said, "All right, Marsh, I'm going to engage you. See what you can discover, and report to me whenever you think you are making progress. Incidentally, keep your eye on the police and see what they are doing. As long as you are working on this job for me, it will be curious to see just how effective our police really are. Now, I suppose you want to ask some questions."

"Yes," said Marsh, "one or two; although as a rule I prefer to start with my mind as free as possible. Mr. Merton has been living at the LaSalle Hotel, I understand?"

"Yes."

"How long has he been living there?"

"Two years."

"I suppose I can find out something of his habits there."

"I think I get your drift, Marsh," said Hunt, with a smile. "I can assure you from my personal knowledge, that Mr. Merton has led a very quiet and most exemplary life. Practically all his evenings have been passed at the University and Chicago Athletic Clubs, and I believe that occasionally he dropped into the Hamilton Club, of which he is a member."

"Why did his wife go to Arizona?" inquired Marsh.

"The boy has weak lungs and the doctors said his life could be saved only by several years' residence in the Arizona climate. Mrs. Merton worships the boy and insisted upon going with him. They have been there two years."

"When do yon expect them back?" asked Marsh.

"I understand the boy is not much better. It might be years before they return, unless the boy should die."

Marsh thought a moment, then said, "You mentioned before that the business could go on without Mr. Merton. I presume he has given you power of attorney?"

"Yes," said Hunt.

"In case of his death, Mr. Hunt, who would be his executors?"

"I cannot see that that has any bearing on the case."

"Perhaps not," said Marsh, "but I am following a line of thought."

"Well," returned Hunt, "if it's of any use to you, I may say that I will be the sole executor."

"It was a very wise move on your part to employ me in this matter, Mr. Hunt, in view of that fact."

"How so?" inquired Hunt.

"Because to the outsider it might appear that you had some personal interest in Mr. Merton's disappearance. You know, sometimes the police are stupidly suspicious."

Hunt sat up with a start. "You have given me food for thought, Marsh," he said. "I hadn't looked at the matter in that light before."

"Well," returned Marsh, "you can now see that my

investigations and reports will be of the utmost value to you. Furthermore, as you have already suggested, I can keep my ear to the ground where the police are concerned, and keep you advised of what is going on."

"Mr. Marsh," said Hunt, rising. "I am very glad you came in to see me. You can count upon my keeping you on this job until everything is settled."

"One more question," said Marsh, also rising. "I noticed a mention of Mr. Merton's country house. Has anyone looked to see if Mr. Merton could by any chance have gone there because of illness, or for some other reason?"

"I know positively he is not there," Hunt replied. "I keep a caretaker on the premises, and occasionally look over the place myself to make sure that everything is all right. The caretaker assures me that Mr. Merton has not been near the place since he closed the house two years ago."

"One thing more, Mr. Hunt, before I go. People sometimes question my right to investigate. Will you give me a line stating that I am authorized to represent you in this matter?"

"Certainly." Hunt sat down at his desk and hastily penned a few lines on a sheet of letter paper, which he then handed to Marsh.

Marsh carefully folded the paper, placed it in his pocket-book, and bidding Hunt good day, went out.

CHAPTER XIII

STARTLING DISCLOSURES

"Why is it that business men, who pride themselves on their astuteness, almost invariably slip up somewhere?" thought Marsh, as he left the La Salle Trust Building and walked north on La Salle Street. This thought was occasioned by the fact that Hunt had neglected to ask Marsh for his address and telephone number. It might be, of course, that the man had taken it for granted that his name and address would be readily found in the telephone directory. Though this explanation passed through his mind, he was more inclined to believe that Hunt's intense interest in the matter, or possibly a newly aroused fear, created by Marsh's reference to the peculiar attitude in which he was placed, had driven the subject of details, out of Hunt's mind.

Marsh had come downtown with the intention of giving his present address, but as the interview progressed, a feeling grew upon him that it might be just as well, at this time, to give some downtown business address. The fact that no inquiry had been made on this point relieved him of the necessity of giving a fictitious address on the spur of the moment. His next step, however, must be the securing of such an address, for it was beyond question that during his next interview with Hunt this information would have to be given.

Marsh glanced over his shoulder at the great clock in the Board of Trade Building, which keeps guard over La Salle Street. It was just twelve o'clock, and he reasoned that the people he contemplated questioning would probably be going to lunch. He decided to spend the next hour, therefore, in securing some sort of office address. By this time he had reached Madison Street, and turning east, looked over the buildings as he passed along, with the idea of selecting one in which a temporary office might be secured. At the corner of Madison Street and Wabash Avenue, he stopped and looked around him. On one corner was the building of a great department store. On the other three corners, big office buildings towered above him. At this corner also here was one of the Madison Street stations of the elevated railroad system. Certainly, it was a most logical location for a man in his supposed line of work, so he entered one of the buildings, approached the starter in front of the elevators, and inquired if he knew anyone who would rent desk room. The starter furnished him with the names and room numbers of two places where he might inquire. The first of these which he visited proved satisfactory. He arranged with the young woman in charge to receive all mail and telephone calls for him and forward these to his regular address. Making a note of the telephone number, he paid two month's rent in advance so as to get the matter off his mind, and returned to the street. The details of this arrangement had taken but a short time, so Marsh went up to the men's grill maintained by a nearby department store, intending to eat a leisurely luncheon in one of the secluded booths.

As he sat studying the menu, a small finger suddenly began to direct his attention to certain items, while a soft voice whispered in his ear, "How do you do, Mr. Marsh?"

In work such as his, startling things were apt to occur at any moment, so Marsh gave no outward indication of his surprise.

"How do you do," he returned, without looking up, but his mind was working rapidly to place the voice.

"What are you doing here?" the voice asked.

"You know better than to ask that question, Miss Allen." Marsh now glanced up with a smile.

The waitress stood up, and to anyone across the room it would have appeared as if they were merely discussing his order, which she was writing on a pad.

"If you are still engaged in counterfeiting work," she said, "I may be able to give you a valuable tip."

"All right," said Marsh, "bring me one of those oyster pies and a cup of coffee. We'll have a chat when you come back."

In a few minutes she was back with his order and talked rapidly in a guarded voice as she placed the silver on the table and arranged his dishes.

"About this time yesterday I had four men at this table and caught snatches of their conversation. I put the facts together about like this: There is a house in the suburbs, near Chicago, where a counterfeiting plant has been in operation. In some way the attention of the police has been attracted, and the whole outfit is to be cleaned out as soon as they think they can get away safely. I have no idea regarding the location, but if you are looking anything up this may be a hint for you."

"Thanks, Miss Allen. It is a hint."

Without further words, she hurried away to attend to another table.

Marsh knew that the girl who had just given him this information was a Government operative, like himself. He would have liked to learn more, if possible, especially descriptions of the men, but he did not know the nature of the work she was engaged in, and feared that any further contact between them might be unwise. For a moment he thought of slipping her his telephone number, but the cautiousness bred by years of experience warned him that telephones, like walls, sometimes have ears. However, he realized that she had told him something worth while. It was unlikely that there was more than one counterfeiting band in Chicago at this time. She had given him a clue, which, like the cuff button, might tie up at any moment with some other developments. Moreover, he now knew that his men were planning to get away and that something must be done in a hurry. After finishing his luncheon he wrote his newly acquired downtown address on a slip of paper, wrapped it in a bill, and then signaled to the girl that he desired his check. He handed her the bill carelessly, and said in a low voice, without looking up, "Something inside for you." She returned in a moment with his change, and as she laid it on the table, said simply, "I understand." Marsh then started out on his search for information regarding Merton.

While Marsh was confident that he would get, the most important part of his information at the hotel where Merton had lived, he decided to work up to that point rather than start there. One reason for this decision lay in the fact that night employees of the hotel could probably give him more valuable information regarding Merton's movements than those on duty during the day. He was only a block from Michigan Avenue, where the clubs at which Merton spent most of his time were located. At these places he secured little information that would further his quest. Merton had impressed the employees of the clubs simply as a quiet man who had dropped in to read his newspaper or book, or have quiet chats with other members with whom he was acquainted. Occasionally he was known to engage in a game of billiards or cards. It was hardly the life of a man who could have such close associations with a gang of counterfeiters as to draw upon himself an act of revenge or the necessity of removing him as a matter of protection. So far as Marsh could discover, Merton had never presented a questionable bill to the clubs. In fact, so far as anyone connected with them could recollect, all payments of any character had been made by check. Marsh had pursued inquiries along this line, because, while almost anyone is liable at one time or another, to be in possession of counterfeit money, such a happening in Merton's case might have possessed unusual significance. It was Marsh's desire to ascertain, so far as possible, if there had been any connection of even a remote character, between Merton and the counterfeiters. Unless some such connection were established, it would be hard to believe that Merton had been the

Sheridan Road victim. Yet the coincidences of this disappearance, the evidences of a crime, and the cuff button initialed "M," possessed too strong a significance to be entirely disregarded.

At the third club Marsh secured practically no information. Merton had been an infrequent visitor and had made little or no impression upon the employees.

Walking north on Dearborn Street and across Madison Street, on his way from this club to Merton's hotel, Marsh thought quickly. If he could not at this time establish a connection, then at least he would try to ascertain the nature of the bait which had been held out to take this man of quiet habits to the North Side at two o'clock in the morning.

On reaching the hotel he found that it was still too early to interview the people he wished to see, so he sat down in one of the big chair in the lobby to pass the time studying the aspects of the case.

Even when his mind was busy, Marsh's eyes were on the alert, and faces met under the most trivial circumstances, photographed themselves upon his memory. His eyes rested casually upon a man who sat opposite him, looking over an evening paper. Gradually Marsh began to feel that the face was familiar. With this realization came the recollection that the man had seated himself very quickly after Marsh had selected his chair. Perhaps his recognition of the face was something that came out of the past, but Marsh always endeavored to connect every noticeable incident with the problem of the moment. It was not long, therefore, before he had placed the man. On coming out of the office building where he had made his temporary address arrangements, he had passed this man standing near the door and also remembered seeing the same man in the grill room where he had lunched. The fact that the man was now seated near him in the hotel lobby was more than a coincidence. Marsh's eyes roved about the lobby with apparently careless interest, and not even the man across from him could have guessed that he had noted anything or become more watchful than before. However, he was planning action. If this man was watching him there could be but one reason - his connection with the present case. If he was connected with this case then he was evidently one of the men they wanted. Marsh intended to be sure.

To change the situation from watched to watcher would involve some quick and clever work. Marsh pondered.

As the bell boy passed Marsh called to him, Slipping a coin into the boy's hand, he said, "I had an appointment here with a Mr. Morgan. See if you can locate him." As the boy started off, calling the name, Marsh watched the man opposite out of the corner of his eye. The man threw down his newspaper, stretched and yawned, while his eyes wandered about the lobby. His movements were of a very casual sort, but to Marsh's watchful eye it was noticeable that his glances were actually following the bell boy seeking Morgan. Marsh was now convinced that his actions were under surveillance, and he next planned how to throw the man off. As he sat intent on this problem, he was startled to heap the bell boy say, "Here's the gentleman, sir," and looking up, Marsh saw Morgan standing in front of him.

The training of both men forbade any indication of the astonishment both felt, but looking into the other's eyes, each read the question there. Marsh jumped up, and holding out his hand, exclaimed boisterously, "Where have you been hiding yourself? I'd about given you up."

"I'm sorry I am late," apologized Morgan, in an equally loud voice, taking the cue. He pulled an adjoining chair close to Marsh and sat down.

"Now," said Marsh, in a low voice, "it is probably needless to tell you not to make your observation too obvious, but I want to call your attention to the man sitting opposite."

Morgan nodded.

"He has been following me all the afternoon," continued Marsh, in the same guarded voice. "As long as I sit here I surmise that he will stay where he is. That will give you time to slip out, pick up one of your men, and get him on the job. I suspect it will be worth while getting a line on him."

"That's easy," returned Morgan. "I'll have him locked up inside of the next ten minutes."

"No," said Marsh, "that would be taking too big a chance."

"On. the contrary," said Morgan, "it would be taking no chance at all. That man has been wanted for a year for putting over a confidence game. I won't mention any names because lips sometimes tell stories to watchful eyes. You just sit here and you'll see something in a few minutes." With that, Morgan went out.

A few minutes later a man strolled through the lobby and approached the stranger. He leaned over and whispered to him and the two went out together. Marsh was congratulating himself that when this man got to Headquarters he might be made to talk to some effect, when Morgan and another man, whom Marsh easily recognized as a detective, approached.

"Where in blazes did your man go?" exclaimed Morgan.

Marsh stared for a moment. "Why I thought your man got him," he said. "Somebody came in and quietly took him out."

"Good-night!" exclaimed Morgan. "Somebody must have tipped him off." He turned to the man with him. "No use hanging around now. Our bird's flown."

As the man left them Morgan sat down again beside Marsh. "How the deuce did you know I was here?" he asked.

"I didn't," returned Marsh. "I had that bell boy page you to test the man across from me. I never had such a surprise in my life as when you turned up. What were you doing here?" he added.

"The Chief asked me to look into this Merton case. What were YOU doing here?"

"The same thing," replied Marsh.

"Looking up Merton?"

"Yes."

"Well, that's funny. What for?"

"Because I strongly suspect he is the murdered man in our case."

Morgan gasped.

CHAPTER XIV

THE NIGHT CALL

As Morgan recovered from his astonishment, Marsh anticipated some leading questions. He headed these off at this time, by saying, "In this case, conditions seem to be somewhat reversed; for up to this time we have found practically no one who could be put under surveillance, yet we have every evidence that we are being carefully watched by others. Several incidents have occurred, including the present little drama which convinces us of that fact. There is no question that we should again compare notes as soon as possible, but this is a dangerous place to discuss the case. I came here to question certain people. As they will not be on duty until later there is nothing I can do along that line for a little while. In the meantime, we ought to look over Merton's rooms upstairs. I could not make an attempt to do this, because I do not possess the proper authority without explaining my real connections. You, however, as a city detective engaged on the case, will have no difficulty in making arrangements to inspect his room."

"That is just what I dropped in to do," replied Morgan.

"Then go ahead and make your arrangements," said Marsh, "and when you are ready, let me go up with you. If we meet anyone, remember that I am working under the special authorization of Mr. Hunt, and you and I have just become acquainted."

Morgan went to the hotel office. In a few minutes he returned with a bell boy and nodded to Marsh. Guided by the bell boy, they took an elevator and ascended to Merton's rooms, which they found consisted of a sitting room, bedroom and bath. Obeying instructions, the bell boy at once retired and closed the door after him.

They first inspected the bedroom, giving special attention to the dresser. This contained nothing save the usual supply of clothing, which served no other purpose than to indicate the wealth and conservative taste of the owner. Marsh particularly sought some jewelry that might help to identify the cuff button as the property of the lost man. He found nothing, however, and considered it probable that whatever jewelry Merton owned was on his person.

From the bedroom the two men went to the sitting room, which they hoped would hold greater possibilities, for a desk stood in one corner near a window. A framed photograph of Merton's wife and son, standing on top of the desk, of course had no significance. They then began a search of the drawers and the interior of the desk.

"Probably you have noticed," said Marsh, after a moment, "the disordered condition of this desk."

"Now that you speak of it," agreed Morgan, "I think it is pretty well mussed up."

"I should say," commented Marsh, "that either Merton is very careless, or else we are not the first people to examine this desk."

"Probably the desk has been gone over, Marsh," acceded Morgan. "But you must remember that Merton has been known to be missing for several days and hotel employees, even under ordinary circumstances, are apt to be curious. The point is worth remembering, but I doubt if it is of any importance."

One by one, they examined various letters and papers. A few touched on business subjects, but the majority were of a personal nature. Most of these were from Merton's wife; the others from business men whose well known names placed them beyond suspicion. In one corner of the desk Morgan picked up a sheet containing some notations regarding bond purchases. Beneath this he found a black, leather-covered notebook of a size that would conveniently fit into a vest pocket. One glance into this and Morgan gave an exclamation. "See here!" he cried, calling Marsh's attention to the book. "This notebook has been kept in cipher. These combinations of letters and figures mean absolutely nothing as they stand."

The two men slowly turned the pages, but as Morgan had stated, the matter which the book contained conveyed nothing to them.

"That looks as if Merton had something to conceal, Marsh."

"On the face of it - yes," returned Marsh. "But just glance at this sheet which covered the notebook. From its subject matter I should be inclined to believe that it represented Merton's handwriting."

Morgan nodded and Marsh went on.

"Now, when you come to look at this notebook, even a hasty glance shows a difference in the handwriting. In. fact, now that my attention has been drawn to it, there is really a marked difference."

"Well?" queried Morgan.

"Offhand," returned Marsh, "I would say, that some-body has been keeping a secret record. That person sat at this desk making additional notes. In a moment of forgetfulness, or perhaps the necessity of hasty conce-alment, the notebook was placed under this sheet and later overlooked. There is a possibility that this notebook was left by the person who preceded us at this desk."

Morgan took the notebook and examined it carefully for a few minutes. "In my work," he said, "I have several times run up against ciphers of various kinds. This is unlike anything I ever saw before, and looks as if it would be mighty hard to unravel."

Marsh again took the book and after carefully examining it, said, "I don't pretend to be a cipher expert. In fact, I never waste time on it. We have men both here and at Washington who can read this sort of stuff backward. I'll send this book to them and we'll soon get a key to the cipher."

At this moment, both men became silent and alert. Someone was slipping a key into the lock of the door. Marsh quickly dropped the notebook into the side pocket of his coat. A moment later the door swung open and Gilbert Hunt entered.

He stopped with a start of surprise, but quickly recovered himself.

"You gentlemen gave me a shock!" he exclaimed. "I didn't expect to find anyone here. Already on the job, Mr. Marsh?" he added.

"Yes," returned Marsh, easily. "I never lose any time, and this room naturally should be looked over."

"And this gentleman with you?" questioned Hunt.

"Detective Sergeant Morgan - Mr. Hunt," introduced Marsh. "Morgan is conducting the police investigation." Then he added, with a wink at Hunt. "We met downstairs and I thought we might as well look things over at the same time."

"I see," said Hunt, smiling. "Have you discovered anything?"

"Nothing to which I can attach any great importance at this time," replied Marsh.

"I thought I would come up and look things over," explained Hunt, as he strolled over to the desk and ran his fingers through the papers. The two men watched him with keen attention.

"Seems to be nothing here outside of personal correspondence," said Hunt, turning around.

"Yes," Morgan answered, "those letters appear to be of

a very ordinary character. As far as I can see, there is nothing there that would help us."

"I presume you are working along other lines also?" inquired Hunt.

"Surely," said Morgan. "We have several men on the case now."

"And what have you found, Mr. Marsh?" inquired Hunt.

"Nothing that gives me a lead so far. I will report to you as soon as anything comes to light."

"Better come to my home some evening," Hunt suggested. "We can talk in greater privacy than at the office. You will find my address in the telephone directory. By the way, I believe you neglected to give me your address this morning, and I do not find your name in the telephone book."

"That's right," exclaimed Marsh." I believe I did neglect to do that." Marsh went over to the desk, tore off the corner of a sheet of paper, and wrote down his new address and telephone number. "Here it is," he said, handing the paper to Hunt. "My name would not be in the telephone book as my work necessitates frequent changes of address. One month I am liable to be in California and the next in Europe. For the present, however, you will be able to get word to me at the address I have given you. Naturally, I will seldom be there, but you can always leave word for me to get in touch with you." Then Marsh turned to Morgan. "We'd better be moving along," he said.

"Yes," agreed Morgan, "there's nothing more to be gained here."

After exchanging a few commonplace words with Hunt, the two detectives went out, leaving Hunt in the room. Downstairs, in the lobby, Marsh said, "I strongly suspect that Hunt wanted to be left alone in that room. That's why I hurried you away. The sooner he gets through up there, the quicker he will leave the hotel. I don't want him around while I am looking up the rest of my information. Now, you watch the Madison Street entrance, while I stand across the street on La Salle. When he leaves, the one that sees him will let the other know."

The two men then separated and took up their watch.

Hunt must have made a careful examination of Merton's rooms, because it was not until a half hour later that Morgan rejoined Marsh and informed him that he had seen Hunt enter his automobile on Madison Street and drive away.

"Morgan," said Marsh. "I want to have a talk with you after I get through here. Suppose I come to your apartment tonight?"

"Fine!" agreed Morgan. "I have some information to give you. I'll run up to Headquarters now, make a report, and go right home. You will find me there whenever you are ready."

"And here is a suggestion, Morgan. When either of us calls on the other, the signal will be three knocks on the door instead of pushing the electric bell. I have a suspicion that answering a bell these days will have to be conducted with caution."

"Perhaps you are right," said Morgan. "I'll remember."

Morgan then walked on up La Salle Street, while Marsh crossed over and entered the hotel once more. There was now only one person who might give him a really definite lead - the night telephone operator - and he went straight to her switchboard. Marsh knew that this young woman was probably overfed with smooth talk, so he counted upon getting better results by going straight to the point.

"Good evening," he said. "You are the night operator here, are you not?"

The young woman, who was arranging things before her in a way that indicated she had but recently come on duty, replied in the affirmative.

"Do you remember Mr. Merton, who has been reported missing?" asked Marsh.

"I should say I do," exclaimed the girl. "An awfully nice man. He appreciated good service. Every Saturday night he gave me a box of candy."

"Read this," said Marsh, handing her his authorization from Hunt.

"Oh, I hope you do find out something," said the girl, as she returned the paper to Marsh. "I'd just hate to think anything serious had happened to Mr. Merton."

"All right," answered Marsh, "then you'll be willing to

help me?"

"What can I do?" she inquired.

"Mr. Merton's kindness to you made an impression upon you, did it not?" Marsh asked.

The girl nodded.

"Then you would naturally recollect anything of an unusual nature which might have taken place during the last few days, would you not?"

"Yes... I think so," returned the girl, somewhat guardedly.

"A telephone call late at night?" suggested Marsh.

The girl was busy with her switchboard for a time. Then she leaned back and looked at Marsh. "See here," she said, "I'd do most anything to help find that man, but I can't take a chance on losing my job."

Marsh now knew that he was going to get important information if he handled the matter diplomatically.

"Remember," he explained, confidentially, "I am not a regular detective. I have nothing to do with the city police department. There will be no publicity attached to anything I learn. I am merely looking up confidential information for Mr. Hunt, who, as you know, has charge of Mr. Merton's business."

The girl was again busy at the switchboard, and when at last there came a pause, she looked carefully around to see that no one else was within ear shot. Then she leaned toward Marsh.

"He got a telephone message at twelve o'clock on Monday night," she whispered.

"You mean last Monday?" questioned Marsh. He recollected that Merton
had been reported missing for ten days.

The girl nodded.

"Of course, at that hour," suggested Marsh, "you were not very busy and would therefore be likely to listen in on the wire."

"The very idea!" she exclaimed, indignantly.

"Look here," said Marsh. "If I can rescue Merton from the predicament he is probably in, someone will be handsomely rewarded. Is it not a safe bet that the person who gives me the correct information to put me on the right track, will be pretty well taken care of?"

The girl sat in thoughtful silence.

"And if Mr. Merton should happen to be dead, Mrs. Merton would be very grateful, indeed, to anyone who had helped her learn the truth," Marsh added.

Again the girl looked cautiously about. The hint of an ample reward was having its effect.

"If I lose my job..." she warned, and then again leaned toward Marsh. "I listened in, all right. It was a man who said his name was Nolan. From what I heard I think he used to be a chauffeur for Mr. Merton. He said he was in an awful hole, that he was unjustly accused of theft, and that they were about to lock him up. He asked Mr. Merton if he could do anything to keep him out of this disgrace. Mr. Merton said he would try and asked where he was. Nolan said he was being detained in the apartment of a man named Ames, at some place on Sheridan Road - I forget the exact number."

"Did Mr. Merton go there then, do you know?"

"I couldn't tell you that. He simply said, 'All right,' and hung up the receiver."

"You have given me just the information I needed," said Marsh. "Your job is in no danger if you let this matter rest just between us two. If anyone else should question you, you don't know anything. And above all, forget about me. You get the idea?"

"You bet!" replied the girl, as she turned again to her switchboard.

Marsh left the hotel, well satisfied with his progress. It was now fairly well established that Richard Townsend Merton was the victim of Clark Atwood.

CHAPTER XV

DEAD MEN TELL NO TALES

Up to this time the case had seemed one of the most mysterious with which Marsh had ever had to deal. Now, however, while elements of mystery still remained, he had certain definite clues upon which to work. The little notebook in his pocket might prove to be a key that would unlock the final barrier. The most important thing before him now, therefore, was to secure a solution to the cipher. It was of too important a nature to trust to the mails so Marsh decided to put it directly into official hands. He glanced at his watch. It was after six, and being Saturday, it was likely that these men had left their offices in the Federal Building. At the same time, this was a very busy branch of the Government and it was just possible that someone might be lingering late. Marsh decided to take a chance.

It had been clearly impressed upon him by this time that he was no longer free to come and go unnoticed. At this very moment there might be a pair of eyes somewhere in that hurrying throng on La Salle Street ready to follow his every move. However much they might suspect him, his exact status in the case was probably still a puzzle to them. He did not believe it safe as yet to betray his connection with the

Government. The problem then was to reach the Federal Building without being followed.

Marsh called a taxi, and loudly giving an address on the South Side, was whirled away. Taking out a bill, he laid it on the seat. In a couple of blocks the taxi was held up for a moment by traffic and Marsh stepped hastily out and softly closed the door. He dashed up the street, turned down an alleyway, and half way down the block turned again through another alley that brought him to a different street. In these dark, deserted byways he could have instantly detected any attempt to follow him. A few minutes later he entered the Federal Building, quite sure that any possible pursuers had been thrown off the trail.

He found a hard working official still in his office, and showing his credentials and explaining the object of his visit, Marsh turned over the notebook. Then he slipped out of the Federal Building, and went to a nearby restaurant to get his dinner. After dinner he proceeded by devious routes to keep his appointment with Morgan. Climbing to Morgan's apartment, Marsh gave three raps, the signal agreed upon.

Tierney opened the door, but after an exchange of greetings, put on his cap and passed out into the hall to stand guard.

"Both of us must have important information," said Morgan. "Which of us, shall tell it first?"

"Let me hear your story first," returned Marsh.

"All right," agreed Morgan. "Here goes. My chief information lies in the fact that we now have two men who are undoubtedly connected with Atwood. Both of these men are known to the police, and once we get our eyes on them they will probably lead us to the men we want. It is only a question of hours, perhaps, because every man on the force now has their descriptions and will keep his eyes open. The first of these is Wagner, the man you saw in the hotel lobby. The other is the man who attacked Miss Atwood. With her description in mind, Tierney and I looked over the photographs at Headquarters. We picked out a man known as 'Baldy' Newman as best answering the description. I took a copy of the photograph to Miss Atwood at her hotel, and while she was not sure, she said it was enough like the man she saw to be the same person. Now, this 'Baldy' Newman is a well known West Side gunman, and we know his usual hangouts. He's a little bit of a shrimp, but an expert with his gun, and therefore a dangerous customer to handle, so Tierney and I were mighty vigilant. We found, however, that for nearly two years he has shown up only twice at his old hangouts. That time ties up in a significant way with your story, Marsh. The last time was early on Monday night, when he showed a roll of money and boasted that he was going to pull off a real job that night. We got this from the bartender, who was mighty sore at 'Baldy.' It seems that our friend had slipped a five dollar bill off his roll to pay for drinks for the crowd, and the bartender still has this bill as a souvenir. IT WAS A COUNTERFEIT. Of course, there's enough in all that to positively tie 'Baldy' up with our case, even if Miss Atwood had not been fairly confident of her identification."

"Now," continued Morgan. "Here's some stuff I brought for you. Sooner or later I believe you can make use of it." Morgan handed some photographs to

Marsh, which he explained as Marsh looked them over.

"The first," he said, "is a photograph of 'Baldy' Newman. He's a good man for you to keep your eye out for, because if he ever shot first it would be all day with you. The second photograph is of Wagner. You have already seen him, but this picture will fix him more firmly in your mind. The next photograph is the one our man made of Atwood's letter. Of course, the letter doesn't tell us much, but the handwriting may. That last photograph is of the hand marks on the dining room table in the Ames apartment. Ordinarily, marks of that kind would tell very little. Our finger print expert, however, called my attention to the fact that there is a scar on the right hand. Of course, a scar in that position might be found on many hands, but if you look carefully at that photograph you will see that the scar forms a sort of acute angle. It is, therefore, not an ordinary scar. The man whose hand we find it on is pretty sure to be one of the men who was in the Ames apartment that night."

"High class crooks like Atwood, while they work alone, are often hard to get, but sooner or later they grow ambitious. They want to be the brains of an organization. Then they call in second-rate crooks like 'Baldy' and Wagner, to do the dirty work. These men are never so clever, and some day, through them, the police get their hands on the man higher up. I think, Marsh, that in this case that is what we are going to do." "You have done well, Morgan," praised Marsh. "I believe on the whole that, while I have secured some valuable information, your work has really brought us the nearest to the man we want."

"That was pretty sharp of on to tie up Merton with the case," commented Morgan. "Of course, when you mentioned it to me I saw its possibilities. Before that I was thrown off the track by the fact that Merton was reported to have been missing for ten days, whereas this supposed crime occurred at two o'clock last Tuesday morning. Why do you suppose that fellow Hunt threw us off like that?"

"Probably he did not do it intentionally," answered Marsh. "Hunt is running the business for Merton, and very likely saw little of him outside of the once. It may have been ten days since Merton had appeared at his office, although only a few days since he was missing from the hotel."

"What made you suspect it in the first place?" inquired Morgan.

"I'll tell you the whole story," said Marsh. "Naturally, I was watching the papers for missing people. When I saw that announcement this morning, and remembered the 'M' on the cuff button, it began to look like a possibility. At any rate, it was worth looking up. To get at the real facts, I knew that I would have to be on the inside, so I presented myself to Hunt this morning as a private investigator who was anxious to get the job of looking up Merton in the interest of his office. I think I got closer to Hunt than any policeman ever would. In fact, I was furnished with inside information that may or may not be significant. This man Hunt holds a power of attorney from Merton, and Merton's will names him as sole executor, Of course, to a criminal investigator that sounds bad on its face. On the other hand, if Hunt possessed such power with Merton there could be no object in his wanting to get him out of the way. Certainly, a man in Hunt's position would not have had dealings with a crook like Atwood. Furthermore, if Hunt did want to make away with Merton, he would more likely do it himself than take the risk of employing others, and so place himself in a position to be blackmailed later. Carrying the thought still further, would a clever man like Atwood take a chance of upsetting his own plans by hiring himself out to Hunt as a common thug?"

"I am positive that Atwood either killed or kidnapped Merton, for I have discovered, through the telephone girl at the hotel, that Merton received a telephone call at twelve o'clock Monday night, summoning him out. That telephone call was supposed to come from the Ames apartment. At two o'clock Tuesday morning the shot was fired in that apartment and Merton has not been seen since. We know definitely that Atwood occupies the apartment across the hall, but at this time I cannot see any possible connection between the two men. Hunt is evidently nervous, because it is my opinion that he used undue influence over Merton, and this disappearance has placed him in a peculiar position. I particularly called this phase of the case to his attention this morning, and subtly suggested that my work would be of value to him in preventing suspicion on the part of the police. That feature was plainly what made him decide to employ me, and I am relying upon it to eventually get further valuable information."

"The little book, with notes in cipher, which we discovered in Merton's room, is somewhat of a puzzle to me just now. It may contain information that will be helpful, or it may prove just a memoranda of business deals. We must not overlook the fact that a man in

Merton's line of work, and the men with whom he did business, have many big plans which must be kept secret until they are launched. That book may have contained data along such lines, and Merton may have simply been referring to it when suddenly called out. You will recall that we found a memorandum regarding business transactions covering the book."

"But," protested Morgan, "there must have been some connection between Merton and Atwood or else Atwood would not have taken such a dangerous step against him. Even you will admit that Atwood was not an ordinary crook. Doubtless, then, every step he took was the result of a definite plan."

"Quite true," agreed Marsh, "but there was never a plan yet that didn't have possibilities of failure. You remember what I have said before; that I believed that shot to have been a mistake. If the shot was a mistake, could not other mistakes have also crept in? Get Atwood and I believe that many things will be cleared up."

"Now there is one thing more," went on Marsh. "I cannot tell you where I got the tip, and the information is only general. Still it helps. There are at least four men in the gang we seek, and their headquarters is in some suburban house near Chicago. The most important point, however, is this: they know positively that we are after them, and have made arrangements to get out at the first opportunity. That means WE must work fast."

Morgan was sitting in his favorite chair by the table. Marsh was seated at the front of the room with his back to the window. At this moment the window glass above his head cracked, a dull thud sounded on the wall across the room, and bits of paper and plaster dropped to the floor.

Instantly Marsh slipped down in his chair, so that his head came below its back, while Morgan's hand shot out and snapped off the electric lamp on the table, throwing the room into darkness. Aside from the slight cracking of the window glass, and the dull crash as the missile struck the plastered wall, there had been no other sound.

Morgan left his chair and felt his way through the darkened room. Opening the hall door he cautiously peered out. Tierney, with his hands in his trouser pockets, was leaning with his back against the wall. He glanced up quickly as the door opened.

"Everything all right, Tierney?" inquired Morgan.

"Sure thing."

"Haven't seen or heard anybody?"

"Nope."

Morgan closed the door and moved back into the room.

"'Dead men tell no tales'," said Marsh, lightly.

"Was it that, or just a warning?" questioned Morgan.

"People do not go to all that trouble just to deliver a warning, Morgan. They wanted to get me."

"Why you?" protested Morgan. "I was here, too."

"They couldn't possibly have seen you where you sat, Morgan. On the other hand, my head, sticking above the back of this chair, and showing against the lamplight, made an excellent target."

Marsh now rose and examined the window. "A nice, clean hole," he commented, "and not more than two inches above my head. A mighty good marksman, with a high-powered rifle, evidently."

"Rifle!" exclaimed Morgan. "We didn't hear a sound!"

"Come here," Marsh called. Morgan joined him at the window. "From here you can see the grand stand in the ball park. The upper tiers are on a line with this window."

"But," objected Morgan, "that is too far away for any man to get a good sight; and remember, we heard no shot."

"Don't forget," Marsh reminded him, "that we live in scientific times. With a telescopic sight, and a Maxim Silencer on his rifle, a good marksman could steady it on the back of one of those seats and pick us off at twice the distance without a sound."

"It is very discouraging," groaned Morgan. "To think that we may be picked off before we've even began to get near our man."

"On the contrary," returned Marsh, "it is very encouraging. When a criminal gets as desperate as that you are not very far away from him."

Marsh then pulled down the shades and instructed Morgan to light the lamp once more.

"Seems kind of dangerous, under the circumstances," remonstrated Morgan.

"On the contrary, the man who fired that shot is probably miles away by this time. He is doubtless laughing to think of fat policemen crawling around over the benches up there right now."

"They would have been," admitted Morgan, "if I had been alone. As it was, I left it to you to do what you thought best."

"I have a special reason, however, for lighting the lamp and pulling down the shades," explained Marsh. "It is just possible that another member of the gang is watching out there for me to leave. Pulling down the shades and lighting up will lead him to think I am still here. In the meantime, I am about to slip down your back stairs."

"Where are you going to stay tonight?" inquired Morgan.

"Home, of course."

"I admire your nerve!" exclaimed Morgan. "Sleeping up in that place all alone, with these fellows hot on your trail."

Marsh laughed. "Seems to me they're pretty close to your house, too, Morgan. Aren't you going to sleep at home?"

"Yes," said Morgan, grinning, "but somehow or other that big, half-furnished place of yours seems more dismal and open to the enemy than my little home here with a police station only a couple of blocks away."

"You forget that I have two policemen on guard up there. They've not been ordered off yet. If I were to let my imagination scare me to death, Morgan, I would have been out of the Government service long ago. This experience is no worse than some of the things I went through during the war."

"Now, before I go, there are two matters I should like you and Tierney to look up for me. First, locate a man named Nolan, who was formerly Mr. Merton's chauffeur. Find out what he has been doing for the last week or two; particularly where he was last Monday night. Nolan is the man who is supposed to have telephoned Merton."

"Then try to get a line on Gilbert Hunt; how long he has been with Merton, and things of that sort. I will look for you at my apartment Monday evening. If anything important should happen in the meantime, try to get me on the telephone. Now, I'm going."

As they passed through the apartment, Morgan said, "I'm sorry you didn't meet my mother. She never interrupts conferences, and has gone to bed by this time."

"There will be many other opportunities, I hope," returned Marsh.

By this time they had reached the back door, and after a silent handshake, Marsh slipped quietly down the rear stairs, then through the alley to Addison Street, where he boarded an elevated train and went home.

He was re-assured by the careful way in which the officer on duty in front of his house scrutinized him as he passed, and went upstairs and straight to bed. It had been a busy day and Marsh had many half-formed plans for the morrow.

CHAPTER XVI

THE CLOSED COUNTRY HOUSE

Sunday morning was gray and dark, with low-hanging clouds and a frosty snap in the air that gave the city its first touch of real autumn weather. Returning from breakfast, Marsh lit the gas logs in his fireplace and sat down before their cheery blaze to smoke and think.

Step by step he analyzed and strove to connect the developments of the last few days. The case was strange in many ways. With numerous clues, suspicions circumstances and half-identified people on every hand, there was no one feature upon which definite action could be taken. Atwood was the most elusive criminal he had ever pursued. Never at any time had the man become an actual personality. Like a will-o'-the-wisp, he was ever in sight, yet just beyond reach. While the detectives struggled along tangled paths that led nowhere, Atwood's long arm continually reached out to strike back.

As he thought along these lines, an explanation slowly took form in Marsh's mind. In some of its features it seemed weird and unreal. This, perhaps, was due to the fact that the few definite pieces of information in his possession had to be largely supported and connected by theories and deductions. Strange as the explanation might seem, it nevertheless gave birth to a well-defined plan of action.

In this way the morning slipped by and Marsh was surprised, on looking at his watch, to find that it was nearly noon. He went to his telephone, called the Monmouth Hotel, and asked to speak to Miss Atwood. When the girl answered the telephone, Marsh inquired if she would care to have dinner with him. The invitation was accepted with quite evident pleasure on the girl's part, and Marsh soon left to keep his appointment with her. On his way to the hotel, Marsh stepped into a cigar store, looked up Gilbert Hunt's telephone number, and made an appointment for the evening. Marsh took this precaution of telephoning Hunt from a pay station because a telephone call is easily traced, and he had not yet decided to advise Hunt of his real address.

Jane Atwood joined Marsh in the lobby of the hotel, and the friendliness of her greeting made him glad of his decision to take her on the trip he had planned for the afternoon.

They had dinner at the Edgewater Beach Hotel. It was the girl's first visit to this show-place of the North Side, and Marsh was delighted with her animated interest in everything about her. In fact, he found it hard to believe that this girl, whose bright chatter, sunny smile and sparkling eyes now held him fascinated, had so recently been through such trying experiences. Marsh felt that it was a natural reaction brought about by this diversion, and he long afterward remembered it as one of the happiest hours in a life that had been replete with professional adventure, but barren in the companionship of women of her sort.

As they sat sipping their coffee, Marsh said, "I imagine you have seen very little of Chicago, Miss Atwood?"

"Yes," she admitted. "One takes less interest in things when sight-seeing trips must be made alone. You know, I have not seemed to make any friends in Chicago."

"When I can spare the time, I want to take you around a little. I am sure that you would enjoy the art museum, for art is akin to music and from what you have told me I know that you are deeply interested in that."

"Yes," she replied, "music has always been my chief companion. The dreams that other girls confide in chums, I have told to my piano."

Marsh lit a cigarette and smoked for a moment in silence.

"How would you like to take a little trip with me out to one of the North Shore suburbs this afternoon?" he inquired.

"I should enjoy it very much," she said.

"Well," Marsh went on, "there is a house out at Hubbard Woods that I want to look over this afternoon for a friend. This is just the day for a stroll along the autumn-leafed roads. I thought perhaps you would like to go with me."

Marsh aided her with her wraps and they walked across to the elevated railroad. At Evanston, a few miles north of the city, they changed to the suburban electric line. The girl took a lively interest in the pretty suburban towns through which they passed, and it seemed to Marsh as if they had but just boarded the train when the conductor called out their station and they alighted.

The place was well named. A lonely little station set down in the midst of thick woods, and a road that wound slightly downhill and away among the trees were all that met the eye. They strolled down this road, passing occasional homes. These were usually well back from the road and almost concealed among the trees. In fact, in some places the house itself was not visible, the only indication of a residence being an ornamental gateway, or sometimes just a simple driveway disappearing into the woods. Fallen leaves rustled about their feet, but much of the foliage remained on the trees. Some of this was still green, setting off the masses of autumn colors that ranged from a sombre brown to vivid reds and many shades of yellow.

"And a great city only a few miles away," mused Marsh, giving voice to both their thoughts.

"It is beautiful," admitted the girl, "but so lonely and quiet. Somehow, one, feels so far, far away from everything. Perhaps the gloomy day affects me, but it seems as if the air were full of some solemn mystery."

At this point Marsh saw a young couple, strolling on the other side of the road. He surmised that they were local residents, and excusing himself to Miss Atwood, crossed over and inquired of the man if he knew where the Merton estate was located.

"Yes," was the reply. "Just keep on south along

Sheridan Road. It won't take you five minutes to get there. The place is on the left hand side of the road. You can't miss it; a gateway with gray stone posts, and there are two big pines inside the entrance to the driveway."

Thanking him, Marsh rejoined Miss Atwood.

"I wanted to find out how to locate the place I was looking for," he explained. "You will pardon my leaving you alone, but it seemed unnecessary to make you cross the street."

"Oh, I didn't mind," she replied.

Marsh's real reason, however, in thus leaving Miss Atwood, was to prevent her hearing mention of the name of Merton. Unquestionably, the girl had read of the case in the papers, and after her own recent experiences might feel a certain timidity in approaching the missing broker's home; especially after her recent mention of how the surroundings affected her.

A slight turn in the road brought them to the driveway which the young man had described. there was no mistaking the two great pines that stood like sentinels at either side, just back of the imposing stone gateway. One of these trees was evidently dead, for it was gaunt and bare, in marked contrast to its companion; and as they paused a moment before the entrance, the wind broke off a rotting branch, which fell at her feet. The gates of iron grill work were standing open, and they turned in and started up the driveway, which was covered with crushed gray stone. The house was farther from the road than Marsh had expected, for it was several minutes before they reached it. As he stood before the great pile of stone and wood, with its drawn shades and general appearance of desertion, Marsh thought of the long, winding road through the woods behind them and half regretted that he had brought Miss Atwood with him. His desire had been to attract as little attention as possible in his inspection of the house. One man scouting around this lonely place would have been a suspicious object. On the other hand, it had seemed to him that a man and woman, out for an afternoon stroll, might exhibit an interest in a large country-house without attracting suspicious attention. But now, as he stood there in the gray autumn light, with the wind sighing through the trees about them and a fine snow beginning to drift down, the place seemed to take on an uncanny atmosphere that, even though nothing worse could happen, would have a depressing effect on the girl. It was too late to back out, however. It would be hard to explain a sudden retreat to the girl, and there was no time to be lost in trying to get the information which he sought. Marsh glanced at his companion. She was looking around with evident interest, and he was glad to note that as yet she exhibited no signs of nervousness.

"I understand there is a caretaker here. Will you come up with me while I ring the bell?"

The girl assented, and they climbed the wide steps over which the autumn leaves were thickly scattered. 'whether or not the bell rang, Marsh could not tell, but certainly no sound came to them. He decided to knock and struck the door with the knuckles of his clenched hand. At the first blow, the door moved and swung inward.

A large hall stretched dimly before them. At one side,

Marsh saw a stairway and at the other a high curtained doorway, which probably led to the drawing room. At the bank of the hall seemed to be another smaller doorway, but Marsh could not be sure in the dim light. He was in a quandary. So far as he could see, the house was deserted. Possibly the caretaker was spending his Sunday afternoon with friends, and the door had been closed carelessly so that the latch had not caught. Had Marsh been alone he would have welcomed this opportunity to carefully inspect the house. The girl now blocked such an attempt, for it was obviously unwise, for many reasons, to ask her to accompany him into the house; and he could not consider the idea of leaving her alone, even for a few minutes. There was no alternative but to postpone his visit until the next day.

Marsh stepped through the doorway, pulled the door closed, and tried the knob to see that the door had latched securely. As he turned away, he glanced toward the shrubbery that bordered the adjoining woods. Although he turned instantly to the girl, and started to assist her down the steps, Marsh's quick eyes had noted a man crouching half-concealed in the shrubbery.

As they retraced their steps down the driveway, Marsh kept a firm grasp on the automatic in his pocket while his eyes, without apparent interest, continually watched the trees and shrubbery on either side. They reached the main road without incident and turned north toward the station. Not a word had been spoken as they passed along the driveway, for Marsh had been too intent upon keeping a keen watch to think of words, and the depressing atmosphere of the place had evidently begun to affect Miss Atwood. In fact, Marsh thought that she seemed to brighten as soon as they passed through the gateway.

"Are you in the real estate business, Mr. Marsh?" she asked.

"No," he replied. "What made you think that?"

"You never told me what your business was," she answered, "and your coming out here to look at that house today gave me the idea that you might be interested in real estate."

"No," he said, "I am not interested in real estate," then added, evasively, but not quite untruthfully, "I am planning, however, to go into some sort of business in Chicago."

The fact was that since meeting this girl, Marsh had began to take an entirely different view of life. He looked back upon his wanderings and realized the emptiness of the passing years. It seemed to him now that a man could ask for nothing more than to settle down to some regular employment in such a wonderful city, and go home every night to find this girl waiting for him.

Marsh stepped off the motor bus at Oak Street to keep his appointment with Hunt. He reflected that he had never seen a street so representative of Chicago and its rapid growth. At his back was the great new Drake Hotel and the whole neighborhood was one of wealth and fashion. Yet, as he passed along the street, he noticed tiny frame or brick dwellings nestling shoulder to shoulder with obviously wealthy homes, and here and there the dark, towering structures of old and new apartment buildings. He found Hunt's apartment in one of the new buildings and paused for a moment on the curb to look it over. Though handsome architecturally and modern in every respect, there was a peculiar sombreness about the building, and the bright lamps that gleamed at the entrance but served to exaggerate the dim interior of the hallway.

Not realizing exactly why he did so, but probably responding to an instinct for caution, Marsh strolled back and forth before entering the building. He noted the two dark and narrow alleyways on either side. One of these, reached through a dim, deep recess in the front wall, was evidently the tradesmen's entrance. Marsh then entered the vestibule and pushed the bell under Hunt's name. This was immediately answered by the clicking of the electric door opener. Hunt's man-servant stood at the apartment door, and after closing it behind him, ushered Marsh down a short hall and into the living room. Marsh's quick eye took in the luxuriousness of the furnishings - and something more. He surmised that Hunt was a bachelor. Hunt advanced to meet him with extended hand.

"Good evening, Mr. Marsh," Hunt greeted him, affably. "I hope you bring me some important information."

"I think it will at least be interesting," returned Marsh, as he handed his hat and coat to Hunt's man.

A log fire blazed in a large open fireplace. Before this was a deeply upholstered davenport plentifully supplied with extra cushions, and at either side of the fireplace were large lounging chairs. Hunt called Marsh's attention to these and told him to make himself comfortable. As Hunt seated himself on the davenport, Marsh decided to take one of the chairs near the fire. This gave him the advantage of having the firelight on Hunt's face while his own was more or less in the shadow, for the heavily shaded lamps about the room furnished only a soft glow that made details indistinct.

Hunt clasped his hands and leaning forward rested his elbows on his knees. "Tell me what you found in Merton's rooms yesterday," he said.

"I found absolutely nothing of importance," replied Marsh. It might be splitting hairs, he thought, but it was Morgan who had actually discovered the note-book. "I looked carefully through his dresser," he want on, "and also examined all the papers in the desk."

"And you found nothing of importance, Mr. Marsh?"

"Nothing," replied March, putting as strong a note of positiveness into his voice as possible, for he now began to suspect to whom the notebook had belonged. "The desk contained only personal and a little business correspondence. Morgan and I examined all the signatures. If you looked that correspondence over, as I presume you did, you will acknowledge that no suspicion could be directed at the men whose names appeared there."

Hunt nodded in an absent-minded way and again asked, "Perhaps this man Morgan found something?"

"I would have known if he had," said Marsh, again evasively. "I entered the room with him, and as you know, we left together."

Hunt now seemed satisfied that Marsh had no special information to give him about the contents of Merton's rooms: "Well, tell me just what you have discovered," he said, settling back into a corner of the davenport.

"For one thing," Marsh began, "I know that Mr. Merton is dead."

He leisurely took out his cigarette case, carefully selected a cigarette, and touch a match to it. It was evident, that this act on Marsh's part was intended to give Hunt time in which to think and pass some comment if he cared to. The man remained silent.

"All right, my friend," thought Marsh. "We'll tell you a little more; just enough to make you think - and perhaps act." Then he continued aloud, "I work along somewhat different lines than those followed by the police. For example, I frequently get better results by sitting down quietly in my room, laying certain obvious circumstances before me, and, through what you might call a method of addition, derive an answer to my problem."

"Quite interesting," murmured Hunt.

"And that is the way I have worked out this problem."

"Tell me the details," said Hunt.

"While you reported to the police that Mr. Merton had been missing for ten days, I discovered by inquiries at his hotel that he was in his room as late as last Monday night. In fact, he was seen to leave the hotel at midnight."

"So I have heard," Hunt broke in hastily. "At the time I notified the police I had not seen Mr. Merton at the office for about ten days."

Marsh nodded, and inquired, "I suppose you follow the papers carefully every day?"

"Naturally," was the reply.

"Then," said Marsh, "you probably read about the murder on Sheridan Road last Tuesday morning - the Sheridan Road Mystery, the papers called it."

"Yes, I read about that affair."

"Didn't it make you think?" asked Marsh.

"I don't understand."

"I'll explain," said Marsh. "Mr. Merton left his hotel at midnight Monday. Two hours later a man was murdered in the Sheridan Road apartment. Mr. Merton has not been seen since."

"Well?" queried Hunt.

"I've just been wondering - that's all," answered Marsh, throwing the remains of his cigarette into the fire place. There was a slight pause as he selected another from his case and lit it.

"Mr. Marsh," said Hunt, "you're driving at something. What is it?"

"Just this,". answered Marsh, leaning forward and looking Hunt in the eye. "You hold a power of attorney from Mr. Merton. You are to be sole executor of his estate. Mrs. Merton may not return for years. That's an easy way to get a business, Mr. Hunt."

Hunt adjusted a couple of pillows and settled back again. "Do I gather from your remarks, Mr. Marsh, that you mean to imply something?"

"No," returned Marsh, "I am just stating an obvious situation."

Hunt now leaned toward Marsh. "Have the police arrived at the same conclusions?"

"Have you ever noticed," countered Marsh, "that what the police know usually appears in the papers?"

"You mean by that that the police have not formed the same connection which you have?"

"I inferred as much," returned Marsh.

"Are you thinking of bringing your theories to their attention?" asked Hunt, as he again settled himself back against the cushions.

"That depends."

"On what?" inquired Hunt.

"Yourself."

Hunt remained silent for a moment, then said, "Do I understand that you are making me a proposition?"

"I'm not laying myself open to a charge of blackmail, Mr. Hunt."

"No," jeered Hunt, "I see you're a clever rogue. I might have guessed as much when you offered to investigate this matter for me."

"A man must make a living," returned Marsh.

"This is a cheap way to do it."

"I haven't had your opportunities," snapped Marsh.

"Damn you!" cried Hunt, leaping to his feet and shaking his fist in Marsh's face. "I'll hand you over to the police."

"And lose a good lieutenant, Mr. Hunt?"

"You're a dirty blackguard, Marsh," stormed Hunt. "You've worked your way into my confidence and now attempt to use your knowledge to hold me up. I admit that you've got me by the throat. A man placed in the position which you have made only too clear to me has only one way out. Of course, I could clear myself, but the stigma and suspicion would remain. All right, what's your price?"

Marsh stared in puzzled silence for a moment, as Hunt glared down at him. In some ways the outcome of the conversation was not exactly what he had expected.

"Mr. Hunt," he said, rising, "I'm in this thing for bigger game than a few hundred dollars."

"I told you to name your price," replied Hunt.

"As I told you before," returned Marsh, "I'm not laying myself open to a charge of blackmail. You think the matter over for a day or two; and in the meantime I'll take my coat and hat."

Hunt hesitated for a moment, then struck a bell which stood on a small table by the davenport. A moment later his man appeared with Marsh's coat and hat and assisted him to put on his coat.

"Good night, Mr. Hunt," said Marsh, smiling, and holding out his hand.

"Good night," said Hunt, shortly, turning away and ignoring the proferred hand.

The servant opened the door and Marsh; passed out. He hurried over to Rush Street and into the telephone booth in a nearby drug store. He talked for a few minutes over the telephone and then took a street car for home.

A half hour later an observant person might have noticed a man lingering in the shadows of Oak Street.

CHAPTER XVII

WHAT THE CARETAKER SAW.

Early Monday morning Marsh started for Hubbard Woods, to carry out his investigations regarding the Merton house These investigations must be conducted along different lines from those he had contemplated on Sunday, for his last interview with Hunt had considerably changed his position in the matter. Hunt now regarded him with suspicion, and it might be considered probable that he had even gone so far as to warn the caretaker he had said was in charge, against admitting Marsh.

Marsh intended to have another look at the place, but only a surreptitious one from the cover of the woods. His chief object now was to discover if neighbors knew anything about the place. As he came down the road he recognized the turn, which the day before had brought him directly in front of the gate, so he stepped to the side of the road, and approached the turn with caution, for he did not want anyone who might be coming from the house to find him near it at this time.

As Marsh walked slowly around the bend in the road he saw the rear of a closed car just disappearing between the gateposts. Only the guarded way in which he had approached had prevented the occupants of the car from seeing him. Marsh hurried to the shelter of one of the big stone gateposts and peered around it in time to note that the car was a large, black one of the limousine type. The next minute it was lost to view around a curve in the driveway, and Marsh paused for a moment to reflect. This might be Hunt's car bringing him up for one of the visits which he had said he was accustomed to make. On the other hand, it seemed too early an hour for a man of Hunt's habits. Moreover, Marsh had reason to believe that Hunt's car would be followed; and certainly there was no one else in sight now. Marsh decided that the matter was worth investigating, and turned into the concealing shadow of the woods. He made his way with difficulty through the tangled underbrush, in what he believed to be the general direction of the house. His guess was correct, for the house was before him when he emerged, a few minutes later, from the woods. He was protected from the sight of anyone in the house by a screen of heavy shrubbery, which divided the lawn from the woods.

He found that in his unguided advance through the woods, he had approached the house to the south, so that he saw not only the house itself, but also had a good view of the garage at the back. The car had evidently just been run into the garage, for a man was closing the doors, while another stood nearby. A moment later, the two men approached the house and passed out of sight. Marsh presumed that they had used the back door, which was out of his line of vision. While the distance was too great for him to see the men's features distinctly, he knew that neither of them was Hunt, for he was now sufficiently familiar with Hunt's figure to have easily recognized it.

To have seen one man or woman around the premises

would not have surprised Marsh, as he was prepared to find a caretaker in charge. That two men should drive up in an expensive automobile, however, store it in the garage, and enter the house, as if perfectly at home, was a peculiar incident. Caretakers do not usually have automobiles; certainly not expensive limousines. If the family had been away for a few days, it would be natural for the chauffeur, or some of the servants, to use the car. But this house had been closed for two years, and Marsh was under the impression that Merton had not been using a private car. If he had been using a car it was hardly likely that he would have let his old chauffeur go. The telephone conversation, which the girl at the hotel had overheard, between Merton and the supposed Nolan, indicated that Merton had more than a casual regard for his ex-chauffeur, or the man would not have appealed to him.

Marsh's suspicions being now definitely aroused, he decided not to take a chance by showing himself in the open. This might very probably be "the house in the suburbs," and he was not prepared to battle alone with four or more desperate men. Though he lingered for some time in his place of concealment, there were no further signs of life, so Marsh, deciding that he was wasting valuable time, crept cautiously into the woods and worked his way back through the undergrowth to the main road.

The next step was to find a close neighbor. Having twice approached the house from the north, Marsh knew that there was no residence near it on that side. He turned south, therefore, and after going only a few hundred feet, approached a gateway that was similar in many respects to that at the entrance to the driveway of the Merton home. It lacked the tall, distinctive pines, however, and a short distance inside the gate he could see a cozy little gardener's cottage, or lodge. Marsh was well pleased at this discovery, for he had hoped to locate something of the kind. Servants are more easily, questioned, more talkative, and usually in the possession of a larger amount of neighborhood gossip, than their employers. He approached the door and knocked.

"Come in," called a feminine voice, unquestionably Swedish in its accent.

Marsh opened the door and found himself in a room that appeared to be kitchen, sitting and dining room. A small, round table was set for two, and a woman stood near the stove, preparing lunch or a midday dinner. Marsh had not realized how quickly the morning was passing. The woman's occupation reminded him that he was hungry, and also gave him a sudden inspiration. He would offer to buy his lunch here, for people always grow more friendly and communicative over a meal.

"You want my husband? He bane come in a minute," the woman said, when she saw Marsh.

"No," Marsh replied, "I wasn't looking for your husband. I've been walking around the neighborhood, and thought perhaps I could get lunch here. I'll pay you well for your trouble."

The woman smiled broadly. "Dere bane enough one more. Yust set down - one, two minute."

Marsh laid his hat and coat on an old-fashioned couch that stood against the wall, and was about to sit down beside them, when the door opened again and a stocky man entered. His tanned face was expressionless, and the eyes looked dully at Marsh. A lock of light brown hair drooped over his forehead from under a cap, which he wore well back on his head. The cap seemed to be a fixture, for it was not removed while Marsh remained, and the detective had the humorous thought that it might also serve as a nightcap.

"Aye give dis yentleman lunch," explained the woman.

The man grunted, took off his coat, rolled up his sleeves and sat down at the table.

"Not very talkative," thought Marsh. Then the woman told him to sit down at the place she had prepared for him. She heaped the three plates with a stew-like mixture. Marsh did not recognize it, but he liked the flavor. With this, and the fresh home-made bread, a cup of strong coffee, and urged on by a healthy appetite, which his morning in the frosty country air had made keener, he enjoyed his lunch.

To these people eating was just a part of their day's work, and beyond the satisfying of a natural appetite, evidently produced no special feeling of enjoyment. Contrary to his expectations, therefore, Marsh did not find an opportunity to open a conversation. One or two remarks were greeted merely with grunts, so he decided to wait until the business of eating had been completed. The man's food disappeared rapidly, including a second helping, and Marsh was pleased to see him at last take out an old cob pipe and fill it with an evil-looking, strong-smelling tobacco from a dirty paper package. Marsh lit a cigarette, chiefly as a matter of protection.

"Have you lived here long?" inquired Marsh, addressing the man.

"Tree year," answered the woman. The man rolled his eyes in her direction.

"I'm thinking of buying a place around here," continued Marsh. "This house next door seems to be a nice place."

He nodded his head in the direction of the Merton home.

The man and his wife exchanged glances. She laughed, but the, man's face looked as solemn as its expressionless lines would permit.

"Et bane bad place," he muttered.

"Nels - he bane crazy!" snapped the woman. "Crazy widt de moonshane!"

"Moonshine!" repeated Marsh.

"Hootch," she explained. "Ole's hootch."

Marsh laughed, and Nels grinned, his features for the first time showing an awakened interest.

Marsh thought quickly. The woman was evidently the "boss," but she would not talk about something in which she had no faith. On the other hand, the man undoubtedly had some

knowledge of things which Marsh desired to know. He decided to side with the man.

"You don't approve of hootch?" Marsh asked her.

"No - no!" she exclaimed vehemently.

"But it makes a strong man work harder - keeps up his health." Marsh glanced at Nels, who showed appreciation of this defense of home-made strong drink by grinning at Marsh. The Secret Service man decided they would soon be friends, and quietly slipping his hand into his pocket, began to detach a bill.

The woman snorted in protest. "Et make Nels see t'ings. No goodt for him," she said, sharply. Then she rose and began clearing the table. While her back was turned, Marsh quickly slipped a bill over to Nels, winked hard at him, and nodded toward the door. Dull as the man seemed, he apparently understood Marsh's suggestion. He winked back and grinned, but as the woman returned to the table his face instantly resumed its blank expression.

"Well," said Marsh, rising. "I must be going." He drew out some bills and presented one to the woman. "I thank you for the lunch. It was fine. You are a good cook."

When taking his leave, Marsh put special emphasis on his parting with Nels. After closing the door behind him, however, he strolled in a very leisurely way toward the gate, and instead of keeping on along the road he leaned against the outside of one of the posts where he was not visible from the cottage. He had not waited long when footsteps sounded on the crushed stone of the driveway and Nels appeared. Marsh beckoned to him and they walked down the roadway until out of sight of the gate.

"Nels," said Marsh, stopping and facing the Swede, "you don't think I ought to buy that house next door, eh?"

Nels shrugged his shoulders. "Dat bane your bes'ness," he said.

"But I don't want to buy a place that has a bad name. Will you tell me what you think is the matter with it?"

Nels glanced about him, and standing a little closer to Marsh, said in a lowered, voice, "Aye tenk bad men live dere."

"But," protested Marsh, "I thought the house was closed, and had only a caretaker, or someone like that?"

"No caretaker," answered Nels. "Tree - four - five men. House look close, but men inside." Then he added, shaking his head, "Fonny-fonny."

"How do you know all this, Nels?"

"Aye watch. Aye see you yesterday, with yong lady."

Marsh smiled. This was evidently the man he had seen crouching in the bushes, and who had caused him to hurry Miss Atwood away from the house.

"Yes," said Marsh, "I was going to look over the house, but there seemed to be nobody home."

"Men inside," answered Nels, giving Marsh a shock.

"Tell me all about it, Nels," said Marsh, patting the

man on the shoulder, "and I'll give you some more money."

"House close two year. Since den Aye see fonny men - most in night time. Big, black car - no light. House stay close - all dark - fonny - so Aye watch."

"Is that all?" inquired Marsh.

"Aye tell my wife - she say Aye drink too much hootch," grinned Nels. "So Aye don't tell her about deh oder night."

"What night was that?"

"Aye tenk las' Monday night. Aye go see Ole. He have some new stuff - goodt - goodt. Aye stay late - don't see well com'n' home. Aye tenk Aye turn in my own gate and walk - walk - walk - but no home. Aye hear auto com'n' - get out of de road. Et pass me - stop." Nels lowered his voice to a whisper. "Aye bane nowhere near home - in front bad place. Men turn on lights - CARRY DEAD MAN IN HOUSE!"

"How did you know he was dead?" exclaimed Marsh.

"He all loose - so," and Nels endeavored to illustrate by allowing his body to droop limply.

"Then what?"

"Car put in gar-rage - all quiet. Aye get scared. Aye see clear now - Aye run like hell!"

"That's all you know, is it, Nels?" asked Marsh.

"All now - but Aye watch."

"You're a good man, Nels - real smart," said Marsh. "Here's some more money for you. Maybe I'll come to see you again."

"You bane fine man," grinned Nels, as he pocketed the additional bill.

"Good-bye, Nels," said Marsh, "Better not tell anybody about our talk. Your wife might hear about it."

Nels winked knowingly and they parted, Marsh going directly to the station of the electric line and returning to Chicago.

As he approached his apartment, Marsh saw a heavily built man lounging on the steps and chatting with the policeman on duty. Marsh paid no attention to this man, merely nodding to the policeman as he passed, and climbed the stairs to his apartment. But after he had unlocked the door he stood in the hall instead of entering. Presently the man came up the stairs and they entered the apartment together. As soon as the door closed the man said, "I've got that dope for you." He pulled out a long envelope and handed it to Marsh.

"Thanks," said Marsh as he took the envelope. "Things are shaping themselves fine."

"Anything I can do?" asked the man.

"Nothing now," answered Marsh, "but you had better have several men where we can reach them in a hurry. How is Oak Street?"

"No change," was the reply. "Hasn't left the house all day." With that the man opened the door and left.

Marsh opened the envelope. It contained the black leather notebook, a letter, and some typewritten sheets. He sat down and read the letter.

The solution of the cipher code used in the notebook submitted, was comparatively simple and we were able to work it out here. This code was evidently not intended for the transmission of secret messages; it was very probably used exclusively to make notations in this book with the sole idea of maintaining privacy for these memoranda.

Due to the simplicity of the code, it could be easily memorized and therefore used for making hurried notes for quick reference.

To the inexpert person the combination of letters and figures gave a bewildering appearance to the notes, but it did not actually make the cipher any more intricate.

You can readily make up your own key to this cipher by writing out the letters of the alphabet from A to Z. Under these letters you again write the letters of the alphabet, placing the letter A under the letter Z and working backward. By this arrangement, A would stand for Z and Z for A. Below This you again write out the letters of the alphabet, and under these, beginning at Z and working backward, write the numbers 1 to 10, which brings yon to the letter Q. From P to J you write the figures 20 to 26 and from I to A you write the figures 30 to 38. The person using this cipher probably memorized these two arrangements. In writing a word of say six letters, he would use four letters and two figures. To anyone glancing at his notes in a casual way, the system looked intricate, but to him these notes could be read almost as easily as if written in plain English.

Attached to the letter were several pages containing the decoded notations from the book. After carefully reading these, Marsh folded the sheets and started to place them in his pocket. Then he paused, glancing about the room thoughtfully. A moment later he smoothed the sheets out flat and lifting up the corner of the rug, slipped them under it well toward the center. Walking back and forth over the spot several times, he seemed satisfied. Then he turned up one of the chairs, placed the notebook inside of the bottom lining, and putting on his hat and coat, went out.

CHAPTER XVIII

THE ENEMY SHOWS HIS HAND

After returning from supper, Marsh sat down to look over the evening paper. The Merton case, which had replaced the Sheridan Road mystery in editorial esteem, was now retired to an inner page. He read the usual short notice that the police expected to have the guilty parties in custody within the next twenty-four hours, accompanied by an announcement of some of their plans so that the people sought could have timely warning of what to expect. Then he turned to other news of the day and the time slipped by.

About nine o'clock Marsh raised his head and listened. He had distinctly heard two sharp reports, like pistol shots. Motors continued to hum past on Sheridan Road, and he could detect none of the unusual sounds which accompany a disturbance of any kind. As a result of having hundreds of cars pass his windows daily he was used to the crack of bursting motor tires, or the back-fire in mufflers. Marsh's trained ear had seemed to catch something different in the two reports, but perhaps it was only imagination. He resumed his reading.

Three soft knocks sounded on the hall door.

It was the usual signal, and Morgan was expected. Marsh laid down the paper, and going to the door, threw it open. Instantly a small figure leaped into the entrance hall and stood facing him with its back to the living room door. A big army automatic held in a long, thin hand, covered Marsh menacingly.

"Shut the door - QUICK!" snarled the visitor.

Marsh towered above the diminutive figure, and he thought with satisfaction that with his bare hands he could crush it like an eggshell. But it has been said that the invention of the pistol made all men equal. Certainly at this moment the automatic in the small man's steady hand more than offset Marsh's physical superiority. So, though he smiled in contempt, he also diplomatically gave the door a sharp push and it slammed closed.

"Now, we'll go in and have a little talk," his visitor informed Marsh, and slowly backed into the living room.

Marsh followed.

A hasty glance showed the man the location of the big davenport. Backing to this, he sat down, looking smaller than ever, and motioned Marsh to a chair across the room. While Marsh seated himself the little man turned down his coat collar and pulled his cap up from his face. Marsh immediately recognized "Baldy" Newman.

"Now," said Newman, "you and me is goin' to have an important conference on serious matters."

Marsh did not reply. He seemed quite at his ease, and not at all interested. Nevertheless, both his eyes and his brain were actively taking stock of the situation; watching for some slip that might enable him to change their relative positions. Newman was leaning comfortably back on the davenport, his legs crossed and his feet a long way from the floor. Marsh surmised that there would be some delay in getting the latter into action again. The automatic, however, was still ready. Held firmly in one hand, the weight of the barrel was supported in the palm of the other, the back of which rested on Newman's knee. Marsh realized that when he looked at this gun he was staring directly into its muzzle. Obviously, this was a time for watchful waiting only.

"We can't figure where you fit into this here game," Newman began. "You ain't a bull; you don't work; and you don't steal."

Marsh laughed at this quaint appraisal of him.

"Well, what ARE you tryin' to pull off?" questioned Newman, his bright, piercing eyes studying Marsh's face.

"You have me at a disadvantage," returned Marsh. "I do not know what game you refer to in the first place. In the second, I cannot see why the pursuit of my private business should interest you."

"Come on - come on!" remonstrated Newman. "I ain't got any time to waste kiddin' around with you."

"Get down to the point then," advised Marsh.

"All right, I will," said Newman. "We don't mind these bulls. They're bone-heads. I can run circles around any one of them. But you're gettin' too damned close, and we want to know what you're after."

"Thanks for the tip," replied Marsh. "If I were really interested in you, the information you have just given me would be of great value."

Newman eyed Marsh suspiciously for a moment.

"Don't worry," he said. "You're not goin' to bother us much. We've arranged to take care of you, if you won't listen to reason. If you're crooked, just lay off for awhile, that's all, and we'll see you get what's right later. If you really are a bull, or are helpin' these other bulls, then I'm warnin' you to back out gracefully before it's too late. I came here with a flag of truce to give you a chance, and you can save yourself a lot of trouble by bein' on the square with me."

Bargaining with a known crook was not to Marsh's taste. If they were in the dark as to his intentions and his status, let them remain so. He guessed now that the gun in Newman's hands would not be used except as a last resort to avoid personal capture. The man's idea was to have his say, and then go as quietly as he had come, if possible. Marsh's tense watching relaxed somewhat. There was no immediate danger, and the future could adjust itself. He would like to get this fellow now, but if not, then he would get him later.

"It is none of your business what work I am engaged in," said Marsh. "Moreover, you can tell your gang for me to go straight to hell. Now, take my advice and get out quick before you lose the opportunity." Newman's lips parted in a vicious grin.

"You've got nerve, I'll say that for you," he commented. "But you don't know what a hole you're in. We've got more than one string to our bow. If you won't listen to one kind of reason, perhaps you'll listen to another. Now, you're stuck on Jane Atwood."

Marsh sprang to his feet with an oath.

"Leave that girl out of this," he cried, "or I'll beat you to a pulp!"

"Steady, Mister, steady!" exclaimed Newman. "You ain't bullet proof. Handlin' a gun is part of my business, and you won't get two feet from that chair if you make a false move. Sit down and listen to me."

Reason quickly replaced the unthinking rage of the moment, and Marsh sat down as the other directed. But his mind was made up to one thing - Newman would not leave that room now except as a prisoner or a dead man.

"That's the idea," said Newman. "You're helpless as a babe, and you might as well acknowledge it. Now, listen to this. You're crazy about Jane Atwood, or all signs fail. In fact, you probably hope to marry her. She's a classy, refined girl, with a big purpose in life. What's more, she's got peculiar notions of what's right and what's wrong. If she knew her father was a crook, and that he died to escape you, where do you think you'd get off? She'd never have anything, more to do with you, that girl wouldn't. She'd devote her life to somethin' or other to make up for her father's slip - that's what she'd do."

Newman paused, and Marsh ground his teeth and waited.

"Now, my man," continued Newman, "another false move on your part and the facts will be given to that girl, with absolute convincin' proof. There'll be no way of talkin' her out of it. You'll be through - that's all!"

While Newman talked, he had gradually leaned forward, deeply absorbed in the driving home of this final threat. The muzzle of the automatic had also slowly turned until a bullet would now strike several feet to the right. Marsh had carefully watched for this approaching opportunity and now he acted.

Like a flash, he jumped to his feet, swinging his right arm upward and forward as if hurling something at Newman. Instinct was stronger than training. The man's arms were quickly raised to ward off the expected missile. Then, realizing that Marsh was upon him, he endeavored to escape, but the powerful hands had already closed on him. He was swung upward into the air, while bullets from the automatic crashed into the walls, the ceiling and the floor, as he tried to direct its fire at his opponent.

For the matter of a second, Newman was poised in midair. Then Marsh, swept by a fierce and uncontrollable rage, dashed the helpless bundle across the room and it struck with a smashing thud.

CHAPTER XIX

KIDNAPPED

Marsh slowly regained control of himself as he stood staring at the crumpled figure. Striding across the room, he bent over Newman. The man was breathing heavily, and his eyes had a dazed glare. Although he was not unconscious in the full sense of the word, it seemed probable that it would be some time before Newman could start any more trouble. Marsh decided, however, that it would be safer to provide against future possibilities, so he drew Newman's hands together and snapped on a pair of handcuffs.

Suddenly Marsh realized that his doorbell was ringing furiously. This time he took no chances, and his automatic was in his hand ready for instant use when he opened the door. He found Morgan and Tierney in the hall.

"For God's sake, what's the matter?" cried Morgan.

By this time Marsh had recovered his calm and easy manner. "I had a visitor," he said, smiling, and slipping his automatic back into his pocket. "Come in."

The two men passed through to the living room and Marsh closed the door and followed.

"Where did he go?" asked Morgan, as Marsh entered the room.

"There it is," said Marsh, contemptuously, nodding toward Newman.

Morgan and Tierney hurried to the man and straightened him out on his back. Newman was still too dazed to do more than roll his eyes at them.

"'Baldy' Newman!" exclaimed Morgan, looking up at Marsh. "How did you get him?"

Marsh briefly explained the incident. "And what beats me," he concluded, "is how he got by the policeman at the door."

"By a well-laid plan, Marsh. We were talking about it to the patrolman when the shooting began. That was the first we realized what the scheme had been."

"What was it?" inquired Marsh. "I thought I heard a couple of shots sometime ago, but as nothing seemed to happen afterward, I concluded it was just somebody's tire."

"You heard shots, all right," returned Morgan. "It seems that an auto stopped on Lawrence Avenue in front of the alleyway. Someone in the car fired two shots at the policeman on guard there. He immediately started for the car, and the man in front, who had also heard the shots, joined him. Naturally the car was out of sight before they had run half a block, and so they returned to their posts. They didn't even get the number of the license, although I suppose it would have been of little use if they had. When you look those things up you generally find that the car has been stolen from some respectable citizen."

"Tierney and I arrived just after the patrolmen got back to the building, and the man in front told us about it. I was puzzled over just what the game was until we heard the shooting up here. Then I guessed that they had only drawn off the policemen so as to let someone get in, so Tierney and I beat it up the stairs as fast as we could. When you took so long to answer the door, we thought you were gone, sure."

"Well, the little rat did have me wondering for a few minutes," admitted Marsh. "If he had really come to kill me I think he could have got me, all right. But the fact was, he just came to warn me, and intended to use his gun only as a last resort. Under such circumstances, if you can only keep them talking long enough, they get careless. You can see what happened to 'Baldy' because he stayed too long."

"He'll have a long stay somewhere else now," commented Tierney, cheerfully.

"And we'll make him talk same more before we get through with him," declared Morgan.

"There is one thing I want to ask of you, Morgan," said Marsh. "Get him out of here as quietly as you can, and don't let the news get into the papers. We don't want the people who sent him to know exactly what has happened. Just let them wonder for a day or two."

"I get your point," answered Morgan. He then went to the telephone and called the patrol wagon, impressing upon the man at the other end of the wire, the need for secrecy, and instructing him to have the patrol drive up the alley back of the house.

"Now," said Morgan, as he turned from the telephone, "I suppose you want to hear about the information I was to get for you."

"Yes," replied Marsh. "Were you able to get it?"

"All that's worth knowing," returned Morgan. "I turned Tierney loose on this man Nolan, and looked up Hunt myself. You can dismiss Nolan from the case at once. He has a job as chauffeur with a big business man in Milwaukee, and hasn't been in Chicago for a month. At one o'clock last Tuesday morning he was bringing this man and his wife home from an affair at the man's club. Someone simply impersonated Nolan."

"Now, about Hunt. I found that he started to work for Merton as his confidential secretary about five years ago. Merton apparently thought a good deal of him, and gradually put more and more of his business into his hands. About a year ago, he made Hunt his general manager, and Hunt has practically been running the entire business ever since. People in the financial district seem to consider Hunt a fine fellow. What he was doing before he went with Merton I have been unable to find out in such a short time."

"I cannot say that this information helps us out very much," said Marsh. "Your news about Nolan simply confirms the idea I already had - that the Nolan message was a trick. I dug up some information today which looks like the best clue we have had so far. I think that by tomorrow afternoon we'll close in on the men we want.

Telephone me at twelve o'clock tomorrow, Morgan, and I will tell you just what to do."

At this moment they heard pounding on Marsh's back door.

"I guess that's the wagon, Tierney," said Morgan. "Let them in."

Tierney went back through the flat and returned immediately with two policemen, who gathered up "Baldy" Newman and his gun and carried them quietly out and down the rear stairs.

"I'd like to tell the world," said Morgan, "that the West Side's most famous gunman has been captured with a man's bare hands. But we'll keep it quiet if you insist on it, Marsh."

"After tomorrow, Morgan, you will have more than 'Baldy' Newman to your credit. Until then, our success depends on secrecy. Now, remember, telephone me at twelve sharp tomorrow."

With that, the men parted for the night and Marsh, after making sure that all his doors and windows were securely fastened, went to bed.

But twelve o'clock on Tuesday passed without Marsh receiving his expected message, for the very good reason that Morgan and Tierney could not get to a telephone.

These two men spent the greater part of the morning in the financial district in a futile attempt to get further information regarding Hunt. About eleven o'clock

Morgan suggested that they go to the North Side and get their lunch so that after telephoning Marsh they would be close at hand in case he wanted them quickly. They took the elevated to Wilson Avenue, and after leaving the train, turned east toward Broadway. At the corner stood a big, black limousine. The door was open and the chauffeur turned to them and said, "Say friends, will you help me get this guy out of the car? He's too drunk to move."

Morgan saw that a man was lying back in a corner with his eyes shut, and nodding to Tierney, went over to the car.

"I've been driving him for two hours," said the chauffeur, "and I don't think there's any chance of getting my money. I want to throw him out. He's too heavy for me to lift. You two guys look husky, and like good fellows, so I thought maybe you'd lift him out for me."

As this sort of thing frequently came to the attention of the detectives, they did not suspect anything out of the ordinary when they climbed into the car and started to pull the man out of the seat. Suddenly the chauffeur slammed the door and sprang to the wheel. The man in the seat, who but a moment before had apparently been in a drunken stupor, now sat up, and drawing his right arm from behind his back, covered the two detectives with an automatic.

"Sit down," he commanded, "and be quiet."

In the meantime, the car was moving swiftly across Wilson Avenue.

Turning north on Sheridan Road, its speed increased to a terrific pace. Morgan noticed this and hoped that it would attract the attention of the motorcycle police, but they met none of these men and the car soon left the city limits and passed through Evanston.

From here on, the road was quiet and they passed only an occasional car. The man with the automatic now instructed them to hand over their revolvers. After he had these in his possession, he felt Morgan and Tierney over carefully to see that they had no other concealed weapon. Then, keeping them covered with the automatic, he reached out and drew down all the shades in the car so that they sat in a semi-darkness and were unable to see where they were going. Morgan judged that they had been riding about an hour when the car suddenly stopped. The door was opened and a man stuck his head in. The man was Wagner.

"Turned the tables on you, didn't we?" he jeered. Then he stepped back and they saw that he also held an automatic in his hand. "Come on," he said, "step lively. You're welcome to our happy home."

Tierney began to swear, but Morgan jabbed him with his elbow. It would be like committing suicide to show any fight now.

"These bulls ought to travel in regiments for self-protection," taunted the man who had been with them in the car. But Morgan noticed, as he stepped out of the car, that the chauffeur had left his seat and was also standing ready with an automatic. These men might have their little joke, but they were taking no chances. The three men escorted Morgan and Tierney up the steps and into the house. Wagner then directed them to precede him up the stairs. They passed down a long hall and into a big room.

"Make yourselves comfortable," sneered Wagner. "And I might as well tell you that you can make all the noise you want, because the nearest house is so far away they couldn't hear a fog horn. Just try to be nice, good little boys, and maybe we'll let you go sometime."

He backed out of the door and they heard him turn the key.

CHAPTER XX

THE FALLEN PINE

That Marsh escaped a similar fate later in the afternoon was due solely to his individual way of arming himself. For some years Marsh had carried a small automatic pistol, which unobtrusively rested in the side pocket of his coat. When he was outside in weather that required an overcoat, the automatic was temporarily transferred to the overcoat pocket. Marsh did this because a gun was seldom needed except in emergencies. At such times a movement toward the hip pocket, where men usually carry their revolvers, frequently gave the other man an opportunity to act first. Marsh had even carried his precautions in this line a little further, for the automatic was always placed in the left-hand pocket. A movement of the left hand does not receive the same suspicious attention from a criminal. In fact, as he had several times discovered, it was possible to distract the attention by a movement of the right hand while quickly drawing the gun with the left, and at close quarters a gun in the left hand was just as effective as in the right.

When no word had come from Morgan by one o'clock, Marsh decided to look the detective up. He called Morgan's home on the telephone, then the detective bureau, and two nearby precinct stations that Morgan might have been likely to drop into while waiting to telephone him. Morgan's mother said he had left early, and the detective bureau informed Marsh that they had not heard from Morgan again after receiving a report from him early in the day. The stations did not remember having seen the detective for a long time. At each place Marsh left his name, and a message for Morgan to ring up at once if he came in.

Marsh was now in a quandary. He remembered that he had not asked Morgan to look anything up that morning and therefore knew of no place where he might endeavor to obtain a trace of him. The case had now reached a point where immediate action was necessary, yet he could not act alone. Of course, he could have called upon the Secret Service Division at the Federal Building, but he had special reasons for wanting Morgan's and Tierney's assistance at this time rather than that of Secret Service men. After long consideration, therefore, he came to the conclusion that there was nothing he could do except stay by his telephone and wait. It never occurred to Marsh that anything of a serious nature could have happened to the detectives on the crowded city streets. The only plausible explanation of the delay might be that Morgan and Tierney had discovered some new clue which they thought of sufficient importance to follow up before keeping their appointment with him. Marsh accepted this explanation readily, because he realized that there were still many loose ends to the case that would permit of new developments at any moment.

When four o'clock came, however, and there was still no word from Morgan, Marsh decided that something must have happened to the two men. He had had ample evidence of the desperate and daring character of their opponents. To raise a hue and cry in the Police Department would utterly defeat his plans. Whatever he did must be carried out quietly. So far as he knew, at this time, there were only two possible sources of information - one, the house on Oak Street; the other, the closed house at Hubbard Woods. First he would get a report from the man on watch at Oak Street. If nothing had occurred there, he would then carry out his proposed raid on the Hubbard Woods house with some of his own men.

Having reached this decision Marsh put on his coat and hat and went down to the corner of Lawrence Avenue to wait for a bus. A stream of motor cars swept steadily by and when one of these turned into the curb and stopped, Marsh paid little attention to it. He was astounded, therefore, when a man opened the door, and addressing him, said, "Step in and be quick about it!" Marsh gave the man a sharp glance, then noticing that one of the man's arms was extended toward him, he dropped his eyes and saw that the coat sleeve was pulled down over the hand, while the barrel of an automatic projected about an inch from the sleeve. Marsh looked about him quickly. The policeman in front of his house was too far away to be of any assistance, if, in fact, his attention could be attracted at all. In the other direction, the nearest people were two women, one of whom was pushing a baby carriage. He then saw that another man had descended from the driver's seat and was approaching him. Marsh stepped back and his right hand shot toward his right hip pocket. Not that he had any intention of drawing a gun while so carefully covered by the other man, but he had a thought.

"Easy, easy!" cried the man. "You haven't a chance in

the world! Do you want to get bumped off right now?"

Marsh murmured something inaudible and withdrew his hand. The man with the gun signaled to his companion. This man came up and felt around Marsh's hip pockets.

"Aw, he's kiddin'," the fellow exclaimed. "He ain't got any gun at all."

Marsh's thought had been correct.

"All right," said the man with the gun, smiling. "Let's go."

It had flashed through Marsh's mind that what was now happening to him might have also happened to Morgan and Tierney. If such was the case it was more than likely that these men would take him to the same place, and that was just the information he wanted. As for getting him into that place, that was a different matter. To carry out his quickly formed plan, it was necessary for Marsh to sit with his left side away from this man, who would probably join him in the car, so without further hesitation he climbed into the car and settled back in the far corner of the seat. The man followed and sat down at Marsh's right, pulling the door to after him. The other man climbed back to his seat at the wheel and started the car. They went down Sheridan Road, and turning through the next street, made the circuit of the block, returning again to Sheridan Road and moving swiftly north.

After a time the man turned to Marsh, and said, "If you take things easy you'll get out of this with a whole skin, but if you start anything - GOOD night!"

Marsh smiled but said nothing.

"Oh, I know you're a cool customer," the man appraised, "but if you think you're going to put anything over on us this time, you've made a bum guess."

"It's hardly likely," replied Marsh, "that an unarmed man would try any tricks while you sit there with that automatic. The fact is, however, that you fellows are giving yourselves a lot of trouble for nothing."

"What do you mean?" snapped the man.

"I mean that I have already offered you my services. All you had to do was to tip me the word."

The man looked at Marsh suspiciously for a moment. "Do you mean that?" he said.

"I see no reason why you should doubt my word."

"All right," returned the man. "Hand over those papers you've got and I'll drop you out at the next street."

"What papers do you mean?" queried Marsh.

"There you go - stalling again. No use; the boss said to bring you up, and I guess he knows best."

"I don't know where you get that idea about any papers," said Marsh. "I can show you quickly enough that the only papers I have on me are of a personal nature and of no use to anyone else."

"Maybe so - maybe so. But after we get you under lock

and key, we know damn well where we can find them."

Thus the argument continued at intervals until they were far up into the North Shore suburbs. Darkness had fallen and the interior of the car was absolutely black except when they passed an occasional street light or an automobile. As Marsh had told Morgan, if you can only make them talk long enough, they grow careless. Passing under the last street light, Marsh had observed that the automatic was no longer leveled in his direction.

The car was of the limousine type, with a glass partition shutting off the driver so that unless he happened to look around he would not know what was going on within the car. Marsh figured that now darkness had fallen, the driver's attention would be directed entirely to the road ahead, for street lights along the suburban section of Sheridan Road were few and far between.

"It's getting warm in here," said Marsh. He raised his right hand and pushed his hat back on his head. At the same time his left hand withdrew the automatic from his coat pocket and the next instant it was pressed into the ribs of the man beside him.

"One move and you're through!" breathed Marsh in his ear. "Give me that gun!" His right arm came down with the hand closing over the man's automatic. The man started to swear, but stopped suddenly as Marsh warned, "Shut up. This matter is in my hands now, and I mean business!" Marsh slipped the man's automatic into his own pocket, and then brought out a pair of light, steel handcuffs which he immediately snapped on his prisoner's wrists.

"When I get ready," Marsh informed him, "I'm going to step out of this car, and I want you to sit perfectly still until I am gone. If you want to know how good a shot I am, just make a move." Marsh settled back into his corner and the car rolled on.

At last, just as they made a sharp turn, Marsh caught a different sound from the wheels, and he knew they had passed into a driveway. With a last warning to the man, Marsh quietly opened the door on his side and stepped out of the car. In the distance he could hear his late captor's manacled hands beating on the glass of the front windows to attract the driver's attention. There was no time to lose, for they would be after him in a minute.

Marsh sped down the driveway, but before he reached the entrance gate he could hear the hum of the pursuing car, and as he sprang through the gate the car was only a few yards away. Then a most surprising thing happened. Weakened by its rotting fibres and the never-ending battle with the winds, the dead pine, which stood beside the gate, swayed and cracked. The next minute it fell crashing across the driveway in a cloud of dying splinters and dust, effectually blocking pursuit by motor.

Marsh dashed across the roadway and concealed himself in the underbrush. The falling pine had identified the place to Marsh as quickly as if the men had told him its name. He was facing the entrance to the house in Hubbard Woods.

The driver of the pursuing car had switched on the

powerful headlights to aid him in locating the fugitive. These lights warned him of the fallen pine blocking the road. Marsh could hear the grinding of the emergency brake; and the hum of the motor died away as the man "killed" his engine in his effort to make a quick stop. So swiftly had the car been moving, however, that it struck the log with a tremendous impact which echoed through the still woods. The front wheels scattered far and wide, and the body of the car climbed up and rested on the pine log.

The two men, although probably well shaken up by the accident, jumped hastily from the car and rushed into the roadway. The headlights were shining directly on Marsh and for a moment he thought the men might discover him among the bushes. Standing in the glare, however, they were partially blinded and the manacled man, realizing this, turned to the other.

"Shut off those damn lights. He'll take a pot-shot at us before we can see him."

The driver leaped back to the car, shut off the lights, and then returned to his companion.

"Not much danger," he said. "The guy's probably making a quick getaway."

"Hell!" the manacled man exclaimed, "the boss'll skin us alive."

"The boss be damned!" exclaimed the other. "This guy'll have the bulls on us if we don't get him, and the boss won't be ready for the getaway until Thursday."

"We've got to get him!" declared the manacled man.

"He can't run all the way to Chicago. I figure he made for either the electric line or the railroad station. You beat it up there quick and see if you can get him."

"All right," agreed the driver. "And you run down the road."

"Where do you get that stuff?" exclaimed the other, holding up his manacled hands. "I'm no good with these bracelets on. It's all up to you now. You're wasting time. Beat it!"

The driver started up the road at a run and Marsh listened to the rapid beat of his footfalls until they disappeared in the distance. Then he cautiously crept out of the bushes and approached the other man. It was so dark that Marsh could barely make out the man's form as it was outlined against the gray of one of the gateposts. Consequently, the man did not discover him until Marsh's hand was on his arm.

"That you, Wagner?" he gasped.

Marsh laughed. "Don't make me talk," he said. "I'm all out of breath making that getaway your friend spoke of."

"Hell!" the other man groaned, expressively.

"It sure is - for you," replied Marsh. "Now, just lie down in the road while I tie your feet."

The man turned to run, probably hoping to escape in the darkness. Marsh's hand still gripped his arm and with a quick movement of his foot, Marsh threw the man down; then unbuckled the belt around the fellow's waist and proceeded to secure his feet with it. As Marsh rose to a standing position a voice close at hand, said, "That'll be all for you. Throw up your hands!"

Marsh did not move.

"I said, put up your hands," repeated the voice.

"They are up," replied Marsh, counting on the darkness.

"Don't kid me!" The speaker suddenly, flashed an electric pocket lamp on Marsh. By its gleam Marsh saw the sparkle of a revolver and wisely put his hands over his head.

The man was standing in front of thick shrubbery. At this moment, Marsh saw, by the dim glow of the pocket lamp, two hands slip from the shrubbery and close about the man's throat. The lamp and the revolver fell to the ground as the man instinctively raised his own hands to break the hold. But in the darkness Marsh heard his body drop with a wheezing sigh.

CHAPTER XXI

THE CHIMNEY THAT WOULDN'T DRAW

Marsh stood for a moment in puzzled thought. Then he heard a cheerful voice say, "Aye bane got him all right," and he recognized his rescuer.

"Hold him for a minute," ordered Marsh, and he leaped over the pine to the car, returning immediately with one of the robes. With Nels' assistance Marsh wound the robe about the upper part of the man's body, fastening his arms to his side as effectively as if he had been placed in a straightjacket. Then he took the man's belt and secured his feet in the same way he had tied up those of the other man. Marsh next took the men's handkerchiefs and two of his own. Stuffing one into each man's mouth, and tying another around his head, Marsh effectually gagged them into silence.

"Now," he said to Nels, "we'll lay these two fellows out of sight in the underbrush."

When this was accomplished he instructed Nels to follow him, and they cautiously approached the house. As they crossed the lawn, Marsh heard rapid footsteps ahead, followed by the opening of the house door. He immediately dashed in pursuit. In the hall he paused to listen for sounds that would indicate the direction the man had taken. He heard the clicking of a telephone receiver hook and a voice calling, "Hello! Hello!" Leaping through an arched and curtained doorway at his left, Marsh discovered a dim light in a connecting room, and darted to the doorway, drawing his automatic and transferring it to his right hand as he ran. He found himself in the library of the house, and in one corner he saw the driver of the car with a telephone in his hands.

"Drop that phone!" called Marsh, leveling his automatic.

Ignoring Marsh's command, the man hastily gave a number to the operator. It was quite clear what was happening. This man, returning from his fruitless quest at the station, had witnessed the capture of his companions. He was now endeavoring to warn some person; probably the principal, who was the man Marsh particularly wanted. There was no time for argument, so Marsh fired.

The man dropped the telephone and stumbled forward in a heap on the floor. Marsh dashed across the room and replaced the receiver on its hook, hoping that the connection had not been made in time for the man at the other end of the wire to hear the shot. Though the man had fallen, Marsh knew that he had nothing worse than a flesh wound in the arm, because he was sure of his aim. He tied the man's hand with a handkerchief, and his feet with his belt, and left him on the floor. Turning quickly to Nels, who had followed him into the room, and now stood watching, he handed the Swede the captured automatic, saying, "Do you know how to use it?"

"Ya, Aye know;" was the smiling reply.

"All right," said Marsh. "I'm going to search the house. Follow me and keep your eyes open." Marsh hurried back through the front room to the hall, with the Swede at his heels, and he heard the man murmuring, as he went, "You bane fine man."

As they climbed the stairs, feeling their way in the dark, they heard a distant hammering. It came from the back of the house, and Marsh and Nels speeded down the hall. The hammering ceased as they approached the door at the end of the hall. A thin strip of light showed beneath it and Marsh heard familiar voices.

"I tell you somebody's come after us," said one.

"Oh, hell! The man said nobody could hear a foghorn here," replied the other. "What's the use?"

Marsh found the key in the lock, and turning it, threw the door open. There stood Morgan and Tierney in the wreckage of what had once manifestly been a beautifully furnished bedroom. A black opening, through which a strong draft came when the door was opened, showed where once had been a shuttered window. The remains of chairs littered the floor, parts of the bed were scattered around the room, and in the center of the floor was a pile of felt that had once been the stuffing for the mattress.

"My God!" cried Marsh, "what has happened?"

The two men's faces lighted up at sight of him, and Tierney shouted, "What did I tell you, Morgan? I knew that guy would find us."

"He bane fine man," added a voice from the doorway.

"Hello Svenska!" bellowed Tierney. "Who are you?"

Nels grinned as Marsh explained who he was.

"How did you get in? Where's the gang?" rapidly questioned Morgan.

"One wounded and tied downstairs, and two safely tied up by the gate," explained Marsh. "One of the two out there is your man Wagner. Now tell me how you got here."

Morgan gave him a brief outline of their adventures.

"But how did the room get in this state?" questioned Marsh.

"Well, you know Tierney," replied Morgan, with a laugh. "He's a mighty restless individual when you try to shut him up. He demolished all the chairs on the door. We found the window frame and the shatters had been screwed tight to keep us in, so Tierney took the bed apart and used the sides to clean out the whole business. When we discovered it was too far to drop from the window, we tried to make a rope with the ticking of the mattress, but when we tested it, the stuff proved to be too rotten to hold us."

"And the worst of it is," added Morgan, "it was cold enough in here before Tierney broke out the window. Since then we've been freezing. If there's a fire in the house, lead us to it."

"I don't think there is," replied Marsh. "Now that you

speak of it, I noticed a damp chill in the place the minute I came in. Nels," he added, turning to the Swede; "you're a good fellow. I saw a big, open fireplace in the library. Build a wood fire there and we'll warm my friends up."

Nels nodded and started off.

"We haven't any time to lose," announced Marsh, turning back to Morgan. "I expect to find my final evidence in this house, and we've got to get back to town pretty soon. You fellows can warm up a bit and then we'll start a systematic search from the garret to the cellar."

All three then went down to the library where Nels was building the fire. Tierney loudly voiced his approval as the red and yellow flames began to creep over the wood. A minute later, however, he was choking and swearing as the acrid wood smoke rolled out into the room instead of up the chimney.

"Aye fix him," explained Nels. "Chimney cover to keep out draft, mebbe." He hurried out of the room.

A few minutes later he returned with a white face and staring eyes.

"You come," he half-whispered, from the doorway. "Aye see somet'ing."

"What is it?" questioned Marsh.

"Aye don't know - Aye only tenk - come quick!"

"Go ahead," said Marsh, "we'll follow," and with Nels

leading the way they all climbed the stairs. Nels had turned on the electric lights in the halls. They could now see their way clearly as he guided them to the attic and across it to an open window which opened on a wide gutter. They crawled out after him and worked their way along a short distance to the big, old fashioned, outside stone chimney from the library fireplace.

"Yust put your hand in - so," directed Nels, making a motion with his arm.

Marsh reached up and followed the suggestion. Just below the top of the chimney his fingers came into contact with a human head.

"My God!" he cried. "Here's our man."

"Holy Saints!" gasped Tierney.

Then Morgan asked, "What do you mean?"

"I think we've found Merton's body," replied Marsh. "You'll have to help me get him out."

With considerable effort, and hindered by the blackness of the night, Marsh and Morgan climbed the slanting, slate-covered roof and perched themselves on the broad capstone of the chimney. Slowly they loosened the wedged in body, gradually drew it out through the top of the chimney, and passed it down to Tierney and Nels, who crept with it along the gutter and passed it through the attic window. Marsh and Morgan followed them, and under the glow of the one dim electric light, the two men made a hasty examination of the body. It was in a fair Mate of preservation, due probably to the cold air, which had been made especially effective by the draft through the chimney. The identification was made certain when Marsh extracted a card case from the man's coat, in which they found the business and personal cards of Richard Townsend Merton, and Morgan located the duplicate of the cuff button he had discovered in the empty apartment.

The examination completed, Marsh turned to Morgan.

"Do you notice that this man was stabbed, not shot?" he asked.

"Yes," returned Morgan. "That was one of the things I looked to make certain of."

"Now," said Marsh, addressing the two detectives, "I guess this job has warmed you fellows up. We can't lose another minute. You, Tierney, make a careful examination of this attic. It should not take yon long, and you can then join Morgan, who will start now to make an examination of the second and third floors. Nels and I will look over the first floor and the basement. You join us as soon as you get through. If you find anything worth while, bring it down."

Leaving Tierney in the attic, and dropping Morgan off at the third floor, Marsh and Nels passed on down to the first floor of the house. A careful inspection of this floor brought nothing of especial interest to light except that there were no signs of its having been used. The kitchen and the pantry were bare of food, and Marsh could see that neither of the sinks in the pantry and the kitchen, nor the kitchen stove, had been used for a long time.

"I thought you said those men were living in the house," he queried, turning to Nels.

"So Aye tenk," Nels assured him.

"Queer," murmured Marsh. "No fire, no food, and no signs of cooking."

"Mebbe in basement," suggested Nels.

"Well, we're going there now," said Marsh. "Do you know the way, Nels?"

"Aye guess," replied the Swede, leading the way into a long hall that led from the pantry along one side of the house. A short distance up this hall Nels opened a door, and they discovered a stairway leading into the basement. Marsh lit a match and located an electric switch. When he turned this a light flashed on below and they descended the stairs. Here they found a hall leading across the house, with a doorway at the far end, and one on either side.

"Aye tenk," said Nels, pointing down the hall, "dat door go outside - dis one to laundry - dat one Aye don't know."

Marsh opened the last door indicated by Nels, and lighting another match, found it a rough basement containing the heating plant, coal bins, and general storage space. He found the electric light and turned it on. But little coal vas left in the bins, and the thick mantle of dust over the other things in this part of the basement showed that it had been a long time since anything had been touched. The last thing, Marsh looked into the firebox under the heating plant. This was well filled with an ash that had resulted from the burning of papers, but after poking around with a long stick, he found that nothing remained which could in any way be used as evidence.

Turning out the light, they crossed the hall and opened the other door. With a match, Marsh found a wall switch close to the door, and snapping this, the room was flooded with brilliant light from several electric lamps pendant from the ceiling, each covered with a green metal shade.

Here was the solution of the deserted condition of the upper part of the house. That part of the house had been left intentionally deserted, for all the men's activities had been centered in this room. It was a large, square room that had been the laundry of the house. Four cots, standing along one wall, indicated where the men had slept, and several pots on the gas stove showed where they had obtained their heat and done their cooking. Through the glass door of a cupboard, in one corner, he saw cans and packages of food. The table, in the center of the room, was littered with soiled dishes and the remains of a meal.

Large patches of black cloth on two sides of the room marked the probable location of windows which had been carefully covered to keep any light from showing on the outside. But what interested Marsh most was the complete counterfeiting equipment in one corner of the room. A small trunk also stood in this corner, and raising the lid Marsh discovered a large quantity of the five dollar bills he had been tracing over the country for the last two years. What he really sought, however, were the plates, and these were apparently missing.

At this moment Nels spoke. "You like to see dis?" he asked.

Turning, Marsh found that Nels had the cupboard door open, and was pointing to a suitcase, which lay on the floor. It had been previously concealed by the lower part of the door.

"You bet I would!" exclaimed Marsh and hurried across to the cupboard. He pulled out the suitcase, which was fairly heavy, and tried to open it. It was locked. Nels pulled out a big knife, with a long blade, and began to cut through the leather at the edges. He presently laid back one side of the suitcase, exposing some clothing to view. It was only a thin layer, however, which Marsh threw quickly aside. Under the clothing he found a carefully wrapped package. Tearing off the covering, he saw what he sought - the plates for the five dollar bills. Beneath the package, laid out in a carefully arranged row, were bundles of stocks and bonds.

Here, at last, was the evidence Marsh had sought, and the confirmation of the theory he had carefully worked out.

CHAPTER XXII

CORNERED

Marsh replaced everything in the suitcase, put it back in the cupboard, and closed the door.

"We're through here for the present, Nels," he said.

Shutting off the lights, the two men returned to the main floor. As they entered the library, Morgan and Tierney appeared, having completed their search of the upper part of the house.

"Any luck?" asked Marsh.

"Nothing at all with any bearing on the case," answered Morgan. "How about you?"

"I found all the evidence we need; most of it in a suitcase, which is probably the one Atwood removed from his apartment."

"There goes one of your theories, Marsh," laughed Morgan.

"Which one?" inquired Marsh.

"That Clark Atwood and this man Hunt were not

in cahoots."

Marsh smiled. "What is the proverb?" he said. "'Tis wisdom sometimes to seem a fool.'"

"Now then, Morgan," he continued, briskly, "there's the telephone. You make arrangements to have your men come out and take care of the evidence in the basement, and the prisoners. While you're doing that, the rest of us will bring in those fellows we left out by the road."

Morgan went to the telephone as directed, and Marsh led the others down the drive to the gate. Everything was just as they had left it, and they found the two men where they had placed them, behind the bushes.

"If I'm any example," said Tierney, "these two guys must be near frozen to death."

"That'll cool off their ambition for a fight," replied Marsh.

Marsh placed Wagner, who was the smaller of the two men, over his shoulder, and Tierney and Nels, carrying the other man between them, followed Marsh back to the house. They put the two men in chairs in the library, and lifting the other man from the floor placed him in a chair near them. Marsh then turned to Morgan.

"Have you fixed everything up?"

"Yes, they ought to be here inside of an hour and a half."

"Fine!" commented Marsh. Then turning to Nels, he pulled out a bill and presented it.

"Nels," he said, "we've all got to go into the city. Somebody must watch this place while we're gone. You have a good gun there, so you can stick around until the police come."

"Sure - Aye watch."

"Come on," Marsh called, and the three men started out. The last thing Marsh heard as he went down the steps, was a voice murmuring, "He bane fine man."

Oak Street lay shadowy and deserted, as Marsh, accompanied by Morgan and Tierney, turned into it from Rush Street.

"Wait here for a minute," requested Marsh, as they stopped in front of the entrance to Hunt's building, and he moved toward the dark tradesmen's entrance. As he neared it, a man appeared from the shadows. They held a low-voiced conversation, and Marsh then returned to the others. When the door was opened, in answer to their ring, the three detectives climbed the stairs.

Hunt's man-servant stood at the door.

"Mr. Hunt in?" asked Marsh.

"Yes, sir," replied the man. "I think you were here before, sir."

"Yes, Sunday night."

"Walk right in, sir. Mr. Hunt's in the living room."

Hunt had evidently been reading, but had risen at the sound of voices, for on entering the living room they found him standing by the davenport, with his finger between the pages of a book.

"Good evening," said Marsh.

There was a look of surprise on Hunt's face, but he quickly mastered it.

"I hardly expected to see you here," he observed, significantly. "And who are your friends?"

"Detective Sergeant Morgan, whom you have met before; and his partner, Detective Sergeant Tierney."

Again that astonished expression passed over Hunt's face. He spoke quite calmly, however.

"May I ask the reason for this late call?"

"It's really a continuation of the visit I made here Sunday night," answered Marsh. "My story has had another and more interesting chapter added to it, and I thought you might like to hear it."

"Naturally, I am interested," returned Hunt, smiling. "Will you gentlemen take chairs?"

Hunt's man, who had followed them into the room, now offered to assist them in taking off their coats.

"Never mind," said Marsh, "we shall be here only a few minutes," and the man left the room.

Marsh now seated himself in the chair he had occupied

on the occasion of his previous visit, and Morgan and Tierney took chairs on the opposite side of the fireplace. Hunt laid aside his book and offered them cigars from a humidor. Marsh refused, calling attention to the fact that he was lighting a cigarette, but Morgan and Tierney accepted, and Hunt, selecting a cigar for himself, then settled down among the cushions in a corner of the davenport.

"My story really begins two years ago, Mr. Hunt," said Marsh, "but I will pass briefly over the early part of it by merely saying that at that time I took up the trail of a counterfeiter, known as Clark Atwood."

"Why should you take up the trail of a counterfeiter?" inquired Hunt.

"Because," declared Marsh, throwing back his coat and exposing his badge, "I belong to the Secret Service Division of the United States Treasury Department."

Hunt remained silent and Marsh continued. "Upon the death of his wife in St. Louis, a few months ago, this man Atwood brought his daughter to Chicago and placed her in an apartment on Sheridan Road. Posing as a traveling man, Atwood was busy in other places, and made only occasional visits to his daughter. To maintain a place of safety and refuge in time of trouble, this man Atwood kept his daughter in ignorance of his real occupation. I may say, at this point, that Atwood had made his living by criminal means for many years, and the venture in counterfeiting was simply the latest of his many ways of gaining a livelihood."

"In the course of time it became necessary for Atwood

to get a certain man out of the way. The plans were carefully laid and the stage set. His daughter believed him to be traveling on the road, but after he was sure that she had retired for the night, he quietly entered his apartment, went to her bedroom, and by means of a hypodermic needle, charged with morphine, rendered her unconscious while she slept, so that there would be no chance of her awakening and spoiling his plans. Then Atwood, and a well known police character known as 'Baldy' Newman, entered an empty apartment across the hall by means of a duplicate key. At twelve o'clock, this man 'Baldy' telephoned the victim at his hotel. Newman represented himself as the man's former chauffeur, and appealed for immediate assistance to get out of some trouble he was in. Atwood, and his confederate, then waited in the dining room of this apartment until the victim rang the bell. Newman admitted him and led him into the dining room. There the two men confronted him with revolvers and on the threat of taking his life, forced him to sign a paper."

"After that, the victim made an attempt to escape. He fled to the front of the apartment, closely pursued by the two men. They attempted to make away with him silently, as originally planned, by knifing him to death. The victim brought a hitch into their plans by drawing a revolver and firing one shot before he died. Had this not occurred, it is probable that the murderers' plans would not have been discovered until long after they had made a safe getaway. As it was, the shot merely hastened their actions at the time. The lights in the apartment were turned out, the dead man was carried across the hall, through Atwood's apartment, and down the rear stairs, where he was thrown into a waiting automobile. When the police arrived, a few minutes later, the men believed that they had gotten safely away, without leaving a trace. They did leave traces, however, and from that minute the police never left the trail until they closed in on the men today."

Marsh took a photograph from his pocket. "Among the traces left in that apartment," he went on, "were the imprints of a man's hands on the dining room table. I have here a photograph of those imprints, and among the many identifying marks there is a scar of a peculiar shape."

Marsh returned the photograph to his pocket.

"I am very glad to learn that you have cleared up the murder of my employer, Mr. Marsh," said Hunt. "What seems curious to me, however, is why you should think this man Atwood would want to kill Mr. Merton. Surely Mr. Merton could never have had any dealings with a criminal such as you describe Atwood to be."

"On the contrary, Mr. Hunt," returned Marsh, "Merton had extensive business dealings with Atwood. In fact, he went so far as to place Atwood in a position where he could rob Merton of several hundred thousand dollars worth of stocks and bonds. The transfer of these securities had been taking place for a year or more, and it had reached the point where the greater part of Merton's fortune was in Atwood's hands. It is evident that Atwood's original intention was to step quietly out of sight with this fortune, but subsequent events led him to believe that he could go on in quiet security if Merton were out of the way. That was the reason why Merton was murdered."

Hunt threw the remains of his cigar into the fireplace,

and slipped the hand that had held it down into the pillows of the davenport.

"And you think you have at last located this man Atwood do you, Mr. Marsh?"

"Yes," returned Marsh, calmly, "because I have absolute proof that CLARK ATWOOD AND GILBERT HUNT ARE ONE AND THE SAME MAN!"

Instantly Hunt's hand whipped out from behind the sofa cushions, and the three detectives found themselves covered by an automatic as Hunt stood up.

"Clever work, gentlemen," he said, smiling. "But after leading men of your type around by the nose for many years, you can hardly expect me to stay here and calmly accept defeat now."

"Oh, no," answered Marsh. "we fully expected you to put up a good fight." He slipped his hands into his trouser pockets, and crossing his legs, leaned back, smiling up at Hunt. "Go ahead; what's your next move?"

"My next move," cried Hunt, sharply, "is to leave you damn fools sitting right there. When I didn't hear from my men this afternoon I knew that something was wrong, and my way of escape is ready."

He backed slowly toward the door, keeping the detectives covered with his automatic. When he reached the door of the room, he called, "Everything ready, George?"

"Yes, sir," a voice replied from the distance.

Hunt again addressed the detectives. "I advise you gentlemen to stay quietly where you are for a few minutes. I am going out of the back door of this apartment, and you, will find it difficult to find YOUR way through in the dark - especially as you may meet a shot at any moment. I bid you good evening, gentlemen."

With that, Hunt backed out of sight through the doorway and all was silent. Immediately, Morgan and Tierney leaped to their feet and dashed toward the door.

"Hold on!" exclaimed Marsh, still sitting quietly in his chair, "Where are you going?"

The two detectives stopped in astonishment.

"We're going to get him!" shouted Tierney.

"No need of taking all that trouble," returned Marsh. "My men are ready for him. Long ago a Secret Service man even replaced his driver at the wheel of his car."

As if in answer to this statement from Marsh, they a was a distant fusillade of shots.

"They've got him," said Marsh, rising. "Now we can go."

"If there's no hurry now," said Morgan, "I wish you would tell us the rest of the story."

"What do you mean?" inquired Marsh.

"How did you come to connect these two men, and how did you get that inside dope on the stealing?"

"You know all the incidents," returned Marsh, "and you ought to be able to connect them as I did. The only information I had about which you did not know was that notebook. The book contained memoranda in Hunt's handwriting, which, by the way, closely resembled the writing in Atwood's last letter. Among these were the names, addresses and telephone numbers of the men who worked with him, and showing their different locations during the past year or two. He also made notations of the different stocks and bonds which he took out of Merton's vaults at various times."

"Atwood, you know, took a suitcase at the last moment from his apartment. This afternoon I located a suitcase in the Merton house, containing the counterfeit plates, and the stocks and bonds which I had found noted in Hunt's memorandum book. Naturally, a large part of the story I told tonight was merely surmise on my part, but you can see how near I came to the truth from the way Hunt acted."

"Another interesting point, due to your foresight, Morgan, was that matter of the scar. I studied very carefully the photograph you had taken. Sunday night, when I was calling here on Hunt, I goaded him into a rage, so that he shook his right fist in my face. I had a good view of the scar then, and my last doubt vanished."

"Another point that isn't clear," queried Morgan, "is that paper Merton signed. What was it?"

"I don't know," said Marsh. "That was a wild guess on my part; that he had signed any paper at all. It seemed odd, however, that an experienced financier like Merton would make an employee sole executor. So I decided that before his death, Merton was forced to sign either a new will, or a codicil to his old will, which was dated back some months so as to offset any suspicions."

"And what do you suppose Hunt expected to gain by kidnapping all of us?" again questioned Morgan.

"Don't you see," explained Marsh, "that we were getting too close, and might be expected to spring the trap at any minute. Our disappearance would divert the police into a search for us instead of for them. In the meantime, they could get quietly away and vanish. And besides, I was supposed to have that notebook - the most incriminating evidence we possessed at that time."

"But see here," now broke in Tierney. "Why did you let that guy think he had a chance to get away, when you had the goods on him? The three of us could have nabbed him the minute we came in."

"Tierney," replied Marsh, "there's a little girl up north that I hope to marry some day. You know her - she's Atwood's daughter. If that girl knew that her father was a crook it would break her heart. I didn't intend that she should ever know. I told Hunt that story tonight so as to show him the hopelessness of his position, and thus drive him out to a finish battle with my men. Sooner or later he had to pay the penalty of being a murderer, and I did not think he would allow himself to be taken alive, so I gave him his chance. His death prevents a personal trial and the presenting of all the evidence. The name of Atwood need not now appear in the reports of the case, and the girl will never connect the references that may be made to Gilbert Hunt, with her father."

"One week!" exclaimed Morgan. "Marsh, you complimented me once on twenty-four hours bum work; It's my turn now, to hand it to you for one week's REAL work."

"I appreciate your good intentions, Morgan," laughed Marsh, "but you forget that I have actually been two years on this job. The last week was simply the windup. It was not my superior work - merely a slip in the man's plans that gave me a clue."

"Hell!" cried Tierney. "Cut that modest stuff. A man who could turn the biggest mystery the Department ever had into a CLUE, is some guy!"

CHAPTER XXIII

SUNSET

One of the sudden changes characteristic of the Chicago climate had taken place. The wintry chill had left the air before the advance of a soft, warm breeze that blew out of the west. It might have been early spring instead of late fall.

Marsh waited outside the music school on Michigan Avenue for Jane Atwood. Presently she appeared, and Marsh was conscious of a quickened beating of the heart as he watched the slender, graceful figure approach. He noted the becoming flush, which spread over her features as she recognized him, and he was certain that no woman ever before had such sparkling eyes and so sweet a smile.

"This is a pleasant surprise," she greeted him.

"I knew you had a lesson today," explained Marsh, "and the weather was so fine that I thought you might enjoy a walk before you went home."

"I should love it!" she exclaimed. "I was just dreading the thought of going straight home to that plain little room in the hotel. Hotel rooms never do seem homelike, do they?"

"Most of my life has been spent in hotels," returned Marsh, as they strolled toward the curb. "My parents died before I was twenty, and since then I have led a roving life." He signaled a passing taxi, and directed the chauffeur to take them to Lincoln Park.

Marsh glanced down Oak Street as the car flashed by. The mysterious shadows that hung over the street at night, and the recent tragic incident which had taken place there, seemed almost like a dream to Marsh, as he saw the street stretch peacefully toward the west in the light of the late afternoon sun. Marsh's attention was quickly diverted, however, for at this point the tall buildings, the smoky streets, and the crowds were left behind. At one side began the long line of palatial residences that has brought to this section of Chicago the sobriquet of "The Gold Coast." On the other side lay a strip of park, and beyond that stretched the rolling waters of Lake Michigan, as far as the eye could see.

"This is what I like about Chicago," exclaimed Marsh. "After a day in the hurry and bustle and grind of the business district, you are swept in a few minutes into a region of trees, grass and spreading waters. At one stroke you seem to leave the seething city behind and enter into the wide spaces of the earth."

"You speak like a poet," declared the girl, "rather than a plain business man."

"Perhaps," returned Marsh, in a low voice, "it is because of something new that has come into my life."

The girl's eyes looked into his for a moment, and seemed to read something there, for she turned with heightened color to look out over the lake.

They sat in silence for the next few minutes; then Marsh leaned forward and opened the door of the taxi. "We'll stop here," he called to the driver.

"Have you been in Lincoln Park before?" he inquired, as they strolled north.

"Only to pass through in the bus," returned Jane.

"I think," commented Marsh, "that this is one of the prettiest parks. I presume that those rolling hills are artificial, but they are certainly a relief, after the monotonous flatness of the rest of the city. There is one, just ahead of us, that is the highest in the park. I want to take you there, for it is a place where I have often sat during the last few months, when I wanted to be alone and think."

"I believe," said Jane, "that this is the first time you have really told me anything abort yourself."

"Frankly," replied Marsh, "that is one of the reasons why I suggested this walk today. This favorite spot of mine appealed to me as just the place to tell you something of my story. There it is," he added, pointing across the driveway to a little tree-clad hill. He guided her across the drive, up the winding path through the trees, to an open space on the hilltop, where they found a bench and sat down.

"It is beautiful," agreed the girl.

Several miles of the shore line lay stretched before them, and beyond it miles and miles of blue-green water rolled in, to break into miniature waves against the embankment. The sun had nearly touched the

Paul & Mabel Thorne

treetops behind them, and the gray of evening already lay out over the lake. The distant horizon changed from a deep purplish tint, where it met the water, through many, shades, until it turned to rich gold, where the light of the setting sun fell full upon fleecy clouds that drifted slowly, far up in the air.

"You asked me a few days ago," began Marsh, "about the nature of my business. I did not feel free to tell you at that time, because I was engaged in working out one of my most important cases. That case is completed; and so is my work along that line. I am a detective, Miss Atwood - for the last ten years in the Secret Service Division of the United States Government."

"How interesting," she exclaimed.

"No, you are wrong," returned Marsh. "I thought it was interesting, but I have found out my mistake. It was a wandering, unnatural life, full of nervous days and sleepless nights. No home life, no family, no friends - lacking all the things that really make life worth living. Miss Atwood, the men who work down there in those great buildings during the day, and go to a little home at night, to be greeted by a cheery wife and romping children, are the most fortunate men in the world. Some of them grow restless at times, and may long for what they think is the glamour and excitement of a life like mine. Work such as mine is necessary to the peace, happiness and progress of the world - but I have come to the conclusion that I would rather let the other fellow do it."

"What do you plan to do, then?" the girl asked softly.

"Unfortunately, my training has been along one line

only, and I must stick to that. But I intend to follow it in a way that will permit me to have a home, and some of the things in life which other men enjoy. I have already sent in my resignation to the Secret Service. As soon as it is accepted I plan to open an office in Chicago, to do private investigative work. There is an immense opportunity for this among the thousands of great business houses here. Then I am going to have a home - and," he added, leaning toward her and gazing straight into her eyes, "I want you to help me start that home."

Jane flushed. "What do you mean?" she murmured.

"That I love you," replied Marsh, as he took her small, soft hand in his.

"But you have known me such a short time," protested Jane.

"Jane," he said, "I have watched over you for nearly two years. When you walked along St. Louis streets and entered shops; when you passed back and forth to your music school in Chicago; I was many times close at hand."

She gazed at him in startled surprise. "I don't understand," she said.

"My work took me to St. Louis," Marsh explained. "There I saw you and fell in love. The same work brought me to Chicago, soon after you arrived here, and though you did not know me - probably not even by sight - I was there, watching over you, and worshipping day by day. Perhaps a week is too short a time for you to begin to care, but I had hoped that you would."

"I do care," she half whispered, "but I did not know that you thought so much of me. I have often longed for a real home myself. You know, my own home was never really a happy one. For years my mother was sickly and nervous, and it was I who incurred all the household responsibilities. It has been years since I had the care and companionship that most girls receive from a mother. My father always provided liberally for us, but, he was seldom at home."

"Then we will start a real home together?" he pleaded.

"Yes," she whispered.

The sun sank out of sight and the twilight folded them in friendly seclusion as Marsh took her in his arms.

Choose from Thousands of 1stWorldLibrary Classics By

Adolphus WilliamWard
Aesop
Agatha Christie
Alexander Aaronsohn
Alexander Kielland
Alexandre Dumas
Alfred Gatty
Alfred Ollivant
Alice Duer Miller
Alice Turner Curtis
Alice Dunbar
Ambrose Bierce
Amelia E. Barr
Andrew Lang
Andrew McFarland Davis
Anna Sewell
Annie Besant
Annie Hamilton Donnell
Annie Payson Call
Anton Chekhov
Arnold Bennett
Arthur Conan Doyle
Arthur Ransome
Atticus
B. M. Bower
Basil King
Bayard Taylor
Ben Macomber
Booth Tarkington
Bram Stoker
C. Collodi
C. E. Orr
C. M. Ingleby
Carolyn Wells
Catherine Parr Traill
Charles A. Eastman
Charles Dickens
Charles Dudley Warner
Charles Farrar Browne
Charles Ives
Charles Kingsley
Charles Lathrop Pack
Charles Whibley
Charles Willing Beale
Charlotte M. Braeme
Charlotte M.Yonge
Clair W. Hayes
Clarence Day Jr.
Clarence E. Mulford

Clemence Housman
Confucius
Cornelis DeWitt Wilcox
Cyril Burleigh
D. H. Lawrence
Daniel Defoe
David Garnett
Don Carlos Janes
Donald Keyhole
Dorothy Kilner
Dougan Clark
E. Nesbit
E.P.Roe
E. Phillips Oppenheim
Edgar Allan Poe
Edgar Rice Burroughs
Edith Wharton
Edward J. O'Biren
John Cournos
Edwin L. Arnold
Eleanor Atkins
Elizabeth Cleghorn
Gaskell
Elizabeth Von Arnim
Ellem Key
Emily Dickinson
Erasmus W. Jones
Ernie Howard Pie
Ethel Turner
Ethel Watts Mumford
Eugenie Foa
Eugene Wood
Evelyn Everett-Green
Everard Cotes
F. J. Cross
Federick Austin Ogg
Ferdinand Ossendowski
Francis Bacon
Francis Darwin
Frances Hodgson Burnett
Frank Gee Patchin
Frank Harris
Frank Jewett Mather
Frank L. Packard
Frederick Trevor Hill
Frederick Winslow Taylor
Friedrich Kerst
Friedrich Nietzsche
Fyodor Dostoyevsky

Gabrielle E. Jackson
Garrett P. Serviss
Gaston Leroux
George Ade
Geroge Bernard Shaw
George Ebers
George Eliot
George MacDonald
George Orwell
George Tucker
George W. Cable
George Wharton James
Gertrude Atherton
Grace E. King
Grant Allen
Guillermo A. Sherwell
Gulielma Zollinger
Gustav Flaubert
H. A. Cody
H. B. Irving
H. G. Wells
H. H. Munro
H. Irving Hancock
H. Rider Haggard
H. W. C. Davis
Hamilton Wright Mabie
Hans Christian Andersen
Harold Avery
Harold McGrath
Harriet Beecher Stowe
Harry Houidini
Helent Hunt Jackson
Helen Nicolay
Hendy David Thoreau
Henrik Ibsen
Henry Adams
Henry Ford
Henry Frost
Henry James
Henry Jones Ford
Henry Seton Merriman
Henry Wadsworth
Longfellow
Henry W Longfellow
Herbert A. Giles
Herbert N. Casson
Herman Hesse
Homer
Honore De Balzac

Horace Walpole
Horatio Alger, Jr.
Howard Pyle
Howard R. Garis
Hugh Lofting
Hugh Walpole
Humphry Ward
Ian Maclaren
Israel Abrahams
J.G.Austin
J. Henri Fabre
J. M. Barrie
J. Macdonald Oxley
J. S. Knowles
J. Storer Clouston
Jack London
Jacob Abbott
James Allen
James Lane Allen
James Andrews
James Baldwin
James DeMille
James Joyce
James Oliver Curwood
James Oppenheim
James Otis
Jane Austen
Jens Peter Jacobsen
Jerome K. Jerome
John Burroughs
John F. Kennedy
John Gay
John Glasworthy
John Habberton
John Joy Bell
John Milton
John Philip Sousa
Jonathan Swift
Joseph Carey
Joseph Conrad
Joseph Jacobs
Julian Hawthrone
Julies Vernes
Justin Huntly McCarthy
Kakuzo Okakura
Kenneth Grahame
Kate Langley Bosher
L. A. Abbot
L. T. Meade
L. Frank Baum
Laura Lee Hope

Laurence Housman
Leo Tolstoy
Leonid Andreyev
Lewis Carroll
Lilian Bell
Lloyd Osbourne
Louis Tracy
Louisa May Alcott
Lucy Fitch Perkins
Lucy Maud Montgomery
Lydia Miller Middleton
Lyndon Orr
M. H. Adams
Margaret E. Sangster
Margaret Vandercook
Maria Edgeworth
Maria Thompson Daviess
Mariano Azuela
Marion Polk Angellotti
Mark Overton
Mark Twain
Mary Austin
Mary Cole
Mary Rowlandson
Mary Wollstonecraft
Shelley
Max Beerbohm
Myra Kelly
Nathaniel Hawthrone
O. F. Walton
Oscar Wilde
Owen Johnson
P.G.Wodehouse
Paul and Mable Thorn
Paul G. Tomlinson
Paul Severing
Peter B. Kyne
Plato
R. Derby Holmes
R. L. Stevenson
Rabindranath Tagore
Rahul Alvares
Ralph Waldo Emmerson
Rene Descartes
Rex E. Beach
Richard Harding Davis
Richard Jefferies
Robert Barr
Robert Frost
Robert Gordon Anderson
Robert L. Drake

Robert Lansing
Robert Michael Ballantyne
Robert W. Chambers
Rosa Nouchette Carey
Ross Kay
Rudyard Kipling
Samuel B. Allison
Samuel Hopkins Adams
Sarah Bernhardt
Selma Lagerlof
Sherwood Anderson
Sigmund Freud
Standish O'Grady
Stanley Weyman
Stella Benson
Stephen Crane
Stewart Edward White
Stijn Streuvels
Swami Abhedananda
Swami Parmananda
T. S. Ackland
The Princess Der Ling
Thomas A. Janvier
Thomas A Kempis
Thomas Anderton
Thomas Bailey Aldrich
Thomas Bulfinch
Thomas De Quincey
Thomas H. Huxley
Thomas Hardy
Thomas More
Thornton W. Burgess
U. S. Grant
Valentine Williams
Victor Appleton
Virginia Woolf
Walter Scott
Washington Irving
Wilbur Lawton
Wilkie Collins
Willa Cather
Willard F. Baker
William Makepeace
Thackeray
William W. Walter
Winston Churchill
Yei Theodora Ozaki
Young E. Allison
Zane Grey